Hold the PICKLE

by JJ Knight

Hold the PICKLE

by JJ Knight
the *USA Today* bestselling author of

Big Pickle ~ Hot Pickle ~ Spicy Pickle
Tasty Mango ~ Tasty Pickle ~ Tasty Cherry
Royal Pickle ~ Royal Rebel ~ Royal Escape
Juicy Pickle ~ Salty Pickle ~ Hold the Pickle
Second Chance Santa
The Wedding Confession ~ The Wedding Shake-up
Not Exactly a Small-Town Romance
Single Dad on Top ~ The Accidental Harem
Uncaged Love ~ Fight for Her ~ Reckless Attraction

Want to make sure you don't miss a release?
Sign up for emails or texts at www.jjknight.com/news

Casey Shay Press
PO Box 160116
Austin, TX 78716
www.jjknight.com

Paperback ISBN: 9781938150357
Ebook cover photo by AJR Images
Paperback illustration by Javvani

ABOUT HOLD THE PICKLE

Sharing a one-bedroom studio apartment the size of a postage stamp with a sexy stranger is not my brightest idea.

I need sleep, not temptation.

But I require my own place, stat. I'm a first-year intern at South General Hospital, and when I'm not working twenty-four hour shifts of pure emergency room adrenaline, I need a bed. A good one.

This stranger and I already have a history. We got into such a brawl competing for the first apartment we both looked at, the manager kicked us both out. Nobody got it.

Now there is only one furnished place left.

We both want it, so we strike a deal. We'll share.

She gets the ultra-comfy mattress during the night while I'm at the hospital.

It's mine when she's at work at her family's deli chain.

No problem, right?

Except one evening I get sent home early after a devastating shift, and it turns out Nadia knows a thing or two about handling a crisis.

And once I sleep with her cuddled in my arms, I know I'm in trouble.

Because after we share the only bed in our place, there is no holding anything back.

1

NADIA

This scheme of mine simply has to work.

I circle the main building of the apartment complex I've chosen, looking for a place to park.

There aren't any spots.

It's ten in the morning on a Tuesday. Who lives here but doesn't work on a weekday? Musicians? Night managers?

I finally give up and look along the curb. I find a gap on the street and hop out of my Jeep.

I ought to be working myself. I graduated with my MBA two months ago. My family expects me to take a position with our national deli chain. Not making sandwiches, but on the corporate side.

I'm not sure it's right for me.

That's why I'm here this morning. Getting an apartment and signing a lease in LA will give me a reprieve. I can't be summoned to Pickle HQ if I'm stuck in California.

And I'm going to get a lease, even if this place

doesn't look very appealing. The scraggly courtyard hasn't been mowed or watered in weeks. Trash has accumulated in the corners.

Undaunted, I trudge toward the apartment office. My navy-blue ballet flats disappear in the overgrowth as I arrive at a shady section of the courtyard where the grass hasn't been burned into hell's carpet.

I can't be picky. Furnished apartments are rare. This is one of only two in a ten-mile radius that I can afford with my meager income. Hopefully, it's still available, because the other is only a one-room studio.

I'm nearing the office door when I hear a deep, gravelly voice that hums through my whole body.

"Please tell Gina to look after the spinal trauma patient from last night. I'll check on him myself when I'm back on rotation … yeah, the one with the thoracic injury."

I slow down. A doctor lives here?

The courtyard doesn't seem so bad now. Maybe the landscapers have been negligent, and the manager is beside herself. It has character, a meandering stone pathway cutting between the four squat buildings. I bet it's lovely when cared for.

The voice returns, sending another shiver through me. "I have twelve hours before I come in. See you on the floor."

Oh, he works nights. Maybe that's the reason all the cars are here. South General Hospital is nearby.

A building full of doctors. I could live with that.

I wonder if this one is as sexy as his voice. I peer into the shadows beneath a set of concrete stairs leading to the second level. There's a man standing there, looking at his phone.

He's wearing scrubs! His sandy brown hair is short and spiky, standing up in every direction from him running his hands through it. He has a modest five o'clock shadow, but it doesn't seem on purpose, like he's normally clean-shaven.

He pokes at his phone, then seems to sense my stare because he looks up. His eyebrows lift when he sees me. "Hey," he says.

He spoke. To me!

"Uhhhh. Oh! Hey." *Nice, Nadia. That was articulate.*

But he smiles, and the flash of his perfect teeth is like a light in the gloom. "Scorcher today, isn't it?"

It is *now.* "Yeah. Is LA always like this?"

He steps away from the brick wall. His pale green scrubs can't hide the heft of his chest. A nicely honed bicep peeks out from his sleeve as he grasps the rail of the stairs above him. "I'm not sure. I've only been here two weeks."

He's new here, too!

"I thought SoCal had perfect weather." I force myself not to smooth my pencil skirt or fiddle with my shirt. *Stay cool, Nadia.*

"Perfect *beach* weather." He grins at me. "If you're into sand and sea."

"I am." I find myself smiling back. Something's happening here. Holy hotness, I need to live in this complex, stat!

Before I can ask him about the apartments, his phone buzzes. "I apologize," he says, and he sounds disappointed. Disappointed! "I have to take this. Will I see you around?"

"I hope so!" My voice is a squeak. Oooh, too eager.

But he grins again as he answers the call.

I skip my way to the office manager's door. I should check myself, but my heart isn't listening. I'm useless when it comes to possibilities. And that doctor, new to town, already making eyes at me, is definitely a possibility.

It's a sign. This is where I'm meant to be. Not in New York, working at Pickle Media with my family. Not in Florida at the Dougherty division with my brother.

Here. By the ocean. Sand and sea.

Maybe with a hot doctor by my side!

I turn the knob on the door to enter the office. A woman with thin, puffed-out red hair sits behind a desk piled with folders.

Maybe I can subtly find out who the mystery doctor is, once I've signed a lease, of course. Wouldn't it be wild if we were neighbors? I could bake him cookies after a long shift of *saving people's lives.*

I'm positively giddy.

"Can I help you?" the woman asks, and despite her dour expression and less-than-friendly tone, I slide into the seat opposite her with open excitement.

I'm ready to sign on the dotted line.

My Los Angeles adventure just got a whole lot better.

DALTON

I watch as the woman I met heads out of the courtyard. Her skirt twitches with each step, and I'm mesmerized. Moving here might have some benefits.

"Dalton, are you sure you're getting enough sleep?" Mom's voice is crackly on the other end of the call. "And eating right?"

"I'm good. I feel fine."

"Did you get a place yet?"

"I'm about to head into an apartment office and try to snag one. I only have twelve hours before my next shift."

"Well, good luck, honey, and don't worry about me. I'm managing fine without you."

But is she? I worked a night job throughout med school to help her pay the bills. But even I can't scrape much extra together right now, dealing with LA prices on a first-year intern's salary plus medical school loans. "You'll tell me if you fall behind."

"Not a chance." She laughs. "You let me know what happens."

"Talk to you soon, Mom."

"You better, Dalton."

I shove my phone in my pocket. At least she'll always have a cell phone, since I got a two-line plan. I am so ready to be pulling decent money to help her out. It's been a real struggle since med school. I couldn't work two jobs like I had in undergrad.

I have to kill it my intern year. Not everybody makes it out. I have to. With bells on.

I take long steps as I stride around the corner to the office. There are only two furnished apartments in the area I can afford. This complex has one of them. I can't delay any longer or I might lose it.

The door creaks when I open it. The place feels old, layers of paint making the trim thick and ill defined. A woman with huge, fluffed, orange-red hair sits behind the desk, piles of folders stacked about her.

And, *hello*, the woman I talked to a few minutes ago sits across from her. Maybe she's having trouble with one of her appliances or a water leak.

I'm handy. I could help her out.

Looking around at the dust and chaos of the office, particularly after standing in the squalor of the courtyard, I wonder why this girl lives here. She's well dressed in a narrow skirt, and her dark hair is smoothed into a polished updo. Maybe it's nicer on the inside?

"I'm here for the one-bedroom," I announce.

"Obviously," the manager says. "So is she." She aims a pen across the desk at the younger woman.

The woman turns around and inhales sharply when she spots me. That face. She has the sharp, perfect features of a real-life princess. But the interest she showed earlier melts from her expression as she realizes we're going for the same apartment.

"Hello, again," I tell her.

Her lips tighten. She's not happy about this.

I'm not either. If I hadn't taken those calls, I'd have gotten here first. "I need it," I say, trying not to plead.

"So does she," the manager snaps. "And you're getting on my nerves."

"I'm a doctor."

"We can see your scrubs from here." She shakes her head and returns to speaking to the younger woman. "This is the floor plan. I need first and last month's rent up front. Can you do that?"

"Yes," the woman says, glancing back at me.

Damn it.

But then she adds, "Do you allow pets?"

The manager huffs. "Not on your life. And if I catch you with one, you're out on your can without the deposit."

My heart leaps at that. I don't really want to take the last apartment from this beauty who smiled at me. Surely, if she's asking about pets, she has one. And she got shot down.

Which will leave it for me, free and clear.

But she says, "That's all right. I'll tell the rescue that I'll pause fostering abandoned kittens while I live here."

She rescues kittens?

The red-haired manager cracks her first smile. A well-dressed rescue princess probably trumps an M.D.

I slump onto a chair, wondering if I shouldn't head straight to the other available apartment. But it's only a tiny studio, not a one-bedroom with a separate living space. And it costs more to boot.

I'll give it a few more minutes. Maybe this place won't be good enough for her.

"You want to see it?" the manager asks.

"I do." Rescue Princess stands up.

The manager motions to me. "You can come, too. I don't want to show it twice."

I jump up. "Thank you. Thank you very much."

Rescue Princess doesn't so much as glance my way as she follows the manager out of the office. Yeah, that ended before it started.

The California sun pierces my eyes after the dimness of the room, and I lift my hand to shade them.

The older woman surveys me as she locks the door. "You look like something the cat dragged in. You sure you're not coming off a bender?"

"Just a twenty-four-hour shift in the ER."

The manager harrumphs. I'm not sure if that means she doesn't believe me or if she thinks the marathon shifts are a bad idea. Most everyone does, but it happens anyway.

"Is it legal to work that much?" Rescue Princess asks.

Maybe I can charm her into letting me have the place. Surely she can afford something nicer. She looks like she comes from money.

I give her the grin that worked earlier. "First-years average seventy-two hours a week."

She gasps as we cross the scraggly courtyard where we first met. "That's terrible! How do you care for patients if you're exhausted?"

"They don't," the manager says. "They are heavily supervised. We get a lot of interns from South General in my building."

My head snaps in her direction. "Are there others?"

"Not currently. I threw out the one who rented the unit you're about to look at. He was too buried in med school debt to make rent." She narrows her eyes at me as we approach the side of the building lined with doors. "Are you financially sound, Mr. Doctor?"

Not really, but I say, "I'm good."

"Me, too." Rescue Princess adds her assurance quickly, but I get a hint of uncertainty, like something might be amiss despite her clothes and overall presence.

Maybe she's not what she seems.

We pause in front of a scratched-up door with a metal plate at the base. It looks like it's been kicked a time or two.

"Home, sweet home," the manager says and swings it open.

The smell of smoke hits us. That's not great, but I can always Febreeze the place to hell.

It's modestly furnished with an orange plaid sofa, a dinged-up oval coffee table, and a TV stand. I don't have a stick of furniture of my own, which is why my apartment options have been limited.

"All bills are included," the woman says, leading us

farther into the place. "But I keep an eye on that electric. I'll pound your door if you keep the A/C running twenty-four-seven."

The kitchen isn't particularly inspiring, a sickly sort of beige, but it has the basics, including a dishwasher, stove, and fridge.

"No microwave?" Rescue Princess asks.

The manager rolls her eyes. "It's not the Taj Mahal."

We peek into a bedroom with gray carpet.

A large round stain marks the floor beside a bare mattress on a metal frame. There's nothing else in the room, but the bed is what I need.

Time to grab the bull by the horns. "I'll take it," I say. "I can move in this afternoon."

"Hey!" Rescue Princess protests. "I was here first!"

"And it's clearly not up to your standards," I say.

"What do you know about my standards?" Her cheeks flush pink.

"This can't be good enough for you."

She lets out a huff. "Why does a doctor need to live in a place like this, anyway? I bet those scrubs aren't even real."

Wait, what? "Why would I fake being a lowly intern with a heap of student loans?"

"I knew it," the manager says. "I've got one who's too poor and one who's too good." She waves us toward the door. "Out. Both of you. I have three other people coming by for this place today. You two can live somewhere else."

Alarm bells ring. "But I love it," I say. "This is a great place."

"Yes!" Rescue Princess says. "I love it, too! I'll take it!"

"Nope," the manager herds toward the door. "I know trouble when I see it. And you two are trouble with a capital T! Out you go. Don't bother following me to the office." She pushes us to the sidewalk.

Only when she's taken off across the courtyard do I fully realize what's happened.

I whip around to my new arch-nemesis. "You lost me this apartment!"

Her dark eyes flash with anger. "No, I was the one who could have gotten it! And you lost it for *me*!"

"You're the one who accused me of faking my scrubs!"

"You're the one who's all, 'Look at me, I'm a doctor!'"

"And you're the saint who rescues kittens!"

She glares at me, which only makes her look more beautiful. I've got it bad.

But this isn't about a hook-up. I need a place to sleep.

I whip away from her and stalk toward the office.

She rushes up behind me. "Where are you going?"

"To sweet-talk that lady into giving me this place."

"Oh, no you don't! I'm going to grovel and beg!"

"I don't think so." I hurry faster.

She breaks into a jog to keep up.

We arrive at the office, but when I try the knob, it's locked.

"What the hell?" I twist it harder.

"Great, just great," Rescue Princess pounds on the door.

The curtain moves aside at the window. We both hurry toward it.

Rescue Princess waves at her. "Please!"

"No, me!" I hold my hand to my heart. "I'll be a model tenant."

The woman holds up a piece of paper with the words "I'm calling the police."

"Shit," I say.

Rescue Princess retreats from the building. "I guess this one's not going to happen."

She's right. Good thing I have a backup.

"Good luck, Rescue Princess," I tell her.

"What did you call me?"

I don't answer that as I hurry to my apple-red Jeep, ready to put a deposit on the studio the minute I arrive. It will have to work. I'll cut my grocery budget. Eat ramen. And send Mom less, damn it.

I leap up onto the driver's seat and pat Bernadette's dash between the collection of tiny rubber ducks. "Don't worry, you will never be on the chopping block." My Jeep is a classic, leftover from my dad.

I spot Rescue Princess stomping up the sidewalk. She unlocks the car in front of me, a Jeep that is a newer model of mine in a color they call Earl blue.

Huh. At least my evil opposition has good taste in cars.

I pull out and drive around her, giving a wave that I hope she knows is sarcastic. Good riddance. Faking my scrubs? And who is she, Miss Wear-Designer-Clothes-to-a-Hellhole?

But when she pulls out behind me, then takes my same route, turn for turn, to the next apartment complex, I have a sinking feeling I'm going to see her again, real soon.

We're headed to the same available unit.

The last furnished one for ten miles.

Here we go again.

3

———

NADIA

No, no, no, no, no!

I slam my palm against the steering wheel as I realize Scrubs Boy is pulling up to the same apartment complex as I am. Again.

I lean my head against the backrest as I kill my car. Why is this happening? Why are furnished apartments so rare in LA?

I have to get this place. It's a tiny studio and costs more than I wanted to pay, but I need it.

When I step out of my Jeep, Scrubs stands on the sidewalk, arms crossed over his chest.

It's an impressive chest, even though I'm no longer interested in cuddling up to it.

But he certainly gave me more than a once-over when we first met. He's a boob man. I saw that gaze.

Maybe I can use that?

I'm not a womanly wiles kind of girl. The last time I flirted with a guy, he thought I was fainting.

But I can try.

I attempt a saunter to my walk, only to have my shoe go sideways in a deep crack in the road. I stumble, tilt, and right myself. But my shoe stays behind.

Smooth, Nadia. Real smooth.

I bend down to put the ballet flat back on.

When I look up, Scrubs is watching me.

I try to bounce my step again. I get no closer than two sidewalk squares when he holds out his arms. "Oh, no you don't."

I halt. "Don't what?"

"Don't get any closer with your perfect hair and pretty face and demonic soul."

I spit out a laugh. "Demonic soul?"

"This manager is a man. I talked to him yesterday when I made sure this place was furnished."

"So?"

"I don't have boobs to flash."

My face blooms hot. "Are you saying I'm going to flash him for a lease?"

"I would if I looked like you."

Is that what he thinks?

He lets out a long gust of air. "So, how are we handling this?"

"What do you mean?" I ask.

"We can't go in like this. We could lose this one. And it's the—"

"Last furnished apartment for ten miles," I finish.

He seems surprised. "Why do you need it? You look like you should be shopping on Rodeo Drive."

"Don't make assumptions." Even as I say it, I

wonder if I should have toned down my outfit for the apartment search.

But my cousin Max watched me leave this morning. I'm staying with him and helping him out at his pickle deli while he's wildly busy between bodybuilding competitions and doctor appointments with his wife Camryn. They're expecting their first baby.

If he gets the slightest hint that I'm not moving to some lovely, safe, new residence, he might tell my dad. Or worse, Uncle Sherman, who will summon me to the family business pronto.

Then I'll never get away. And I need to. I must have this studio!

We continue to stand in a stalemate as the heat rises from the sidewalk on the blistering July day.

Finally, he takes a step back. "We have to call a truce. If we argue, we might both lose. Again."

He's right. I extend a hand. "Truce."

He takes it, and despite the fact that he's my sworn rival, my whole body revs up at the warm contact of his palm pressed to mine.

Now that we're close, I see that his eyes are changelings, shifting from green to blue to gray. They reflect me, the sky, the building behind us. I could stare into them for hours.

I realize we're holding hands and jerk mine away. "I suppose I should know your name."

"Dalton," he says as we head toward the office.

"I'm Nadia."

"Well, Nadia," he says. "May the best renter win."

I sure hope it's me.

The air conditioning hits us when Dalton opens the door. A man stands up from behind a desk. This office is much nicer than the last one, organized with bookshelves and file cabinets. There are even plants on the windowsills.

"I'm Evan," the man says. "How can I help you?"

Dalton steps forward to shake his hand. "I'm Dalton. This is Nadia. We're interested in the studio you have."

Evan nods. "Good, good. We just got that one prepped for the next occupant. Have a seat." He gestures to two chairs on our side of the desk.

I sit down uncertainly. I know Dalton meant that we were each individually interested in the apartment, but I think this man thinks we're together.

"I'm also interested," I say.

Evan pauses. "I would assume so."

That didn't fix anything.

Before I can try again, he pushes a printout toward us and says, "Here's the layout."

Dalton and I lean forward to look. It's not much, a single big room with a kitchen in one corner, a bar with two stools, a bed on one side, and a sofa on the other. The bathroom occupies the corner opposite the kitchen.

"Is there a closet?" I ask.

Evan points to a narrow rectangle between the bathroom and kitchen. "That's it here."

Gosh, it doesn't look like it would hold a set of bath towels, much less a wardrobe. I have a ridiculous number of clothes here. My brothers made big fun of the number of suitcases I brought.

But I wasn't sure what I'd end up doing. Working at the family deli? I needed jeans and T-shirts and comfortable shoes.

Getting a desk job with my MBA? Suits and heels.

Being a beach bum? I have a terrific assortment of bathing suits and sandals.

It doesn't matter. I'm out of options.

Evan points to the rent amount in the corner. "Upon move-in, we ask for the first month's rent, plus fifty percent as a deposit."

That's more reasonable than the last place. And Evan seems much nicer.

"But no bills are included," Dalton says.

"Correct."

Oh, that's worse. It means it will be even more expensive. I'm really stretching how far my paltry deli paycheck will go. I'm definitely not asking for money from my family. If they think for even a second that I'm struggling, they'll swoop in and take over my life.

But I have to do this.

"Can we see it?" Dalton asks.

"Certainly." Evan stands, and we follow him out the back of the office to a beautiful courtyard with an actual pool.

Okay, big perk there.

He unlocks a door that *doesn't* look like it was involved in a police raid, and we step inside.

It smells clean. The sofa is gray and nondescript, but seems fairly new. The mattress sits on a pretty white iron frame and is covered with an allergy-protective cover.

The kitchen is bright white, with reasonably updated

appliances. I peek in the bathroom, and it's clean and shiny.

"I'll take it," I say.

"So will I," Dalton throws in.

"Good, good, we can have you fill out the application." Evan leads us back to the door. "Will you file for it jointly?"

"Hold on a sec while we figure that out." I grab Dalton's hand and drag him to the kitchen.

"He thinks we're doing this together, you dolt!" I hiss. "You said it wrong!"

Dalton runs his hands over his stubble. "I see that."

"What are you going to do to fix it?"

"Take the apartment myself."

"You can't do that!" I hiss. "I want it!"

He shrugs. "I guess we can both fill out applications."

That's risky. He could choose Dalton. I tap my foot in irritation. "Why do you need it so bad?"

"I'm sleeping on the floor of my friend's place and with the shifts I'm working, I need a proper bed." He points to the mattress. "That one looks good."

"I'm living with my cousin, and his wife is pregnant!" I almost mention that I need a lease to keep me in LA but then think better of it.

"But you're not sleeping on the floor," he counters.

"That doesn't settle it! It's critical I leave. I can't afford more than this. I'm not sure I can afford this one."

This gets his attention. "I'm not sure I can either, to

be honest. I was hoping to get him to come down, but I can't do that if you want it."

We stand there at a stalemate.

"Whenever you two are ready to come to the office," Evan says, placing his hand on the doorknob.

We don't move.

"What do you do?" Dalton asks.

"What do you mean?"

"For work. What hours?"

"I help out at a deli. Morning and afternoons."

He snaps his fingers. "I work long shifts. I mostly sleep in the morning and early afternoon. That would be while you're gone."

My brain buzzes with this information. "What are you suggesting?"

"Neither of us can afford it alone, but what if we time share it? I sleep while you're at work. You sleep while I'm at the hospital."

"You mean live together?" My face blooms hot. "With only one bed?"

"We won't be in it at the same time."

I cross my arms. "But you were positively ogling me earlier."

He holds up his palms. "I will be hands off. You're my roommate now. Like a sister."

A sister!

Evan clears his throat. "Second thoughts? I had a couple of other calls about this unit."

"No!" we both say at the same time.

"Yes or no?" Dalton asks.

Ooooh. I'm no good at snap decisions. But sharing

would be a lot cheaper. A whole lot. I'd be more free to figure things out.

I have to. "Okay. Let's do it."

"Great." Dalton walks toward Evan. "It's all decided. We're good."

"You work at South General?" Evan asks.

Dalton nods as we step outside, and Evan locks the door behind us. "Just started my internship."

"It's nice to have a doctor around."

Dalton looks very pleased with himself as we head back to the office.

"How long have you two been together?" Evan asks.

I'm about to correct this entire line of thinking when Dalton says, "It feels brand new."

Evan laughs as we pass by the gorgeous courtyard to enter the office to sign the paperwork.

And just like that, I have an apartment. A roommate.

And, if you ask Evan, a boyfriend.

What have I done?

4

DALTON

I'm toast after a twenty-hour ER shift that involved more bodily fluids than the morning after a frat party, and about as much regret on the part of our patients. It was messy, unglamorous work, the stuff an intern's bad days are made of.

But today I have a bed waiting for me, a real one. I don't have to sleep on Jerry's floor or end up the jungle gym for his pair of hyperactive chihuahuas.

Nadia shouldn't be at the new place. I haven't talked to her since we got the keys. But it's a little past nine a.m., smack in the middle of her deli shift, and I have hours ahead of blissful solitary sleep.

I can almost feel the pure bliss of smooth sheets on my cheek.

Sunlight angles into the space as I open the door. It's spotlessly clean, which is good. The stranger I'm living with isn't so much of a slob that she wrecked it in a day.

I look for signs of her, a few clues to who she might

be other than the goddess in a pencil skirt I've known for maybe two hours.

There are blackout curtains on the window and a blue comforter on the bed. Nice. Living with a woman has its perks.

I drop a trash bag and my oversized army duffle onto the floor. For a moment, I run my hand over the name MURPHY stenciled in black on its dark green surface. It belonged to Dad. I lost him a long time ago to complications from a wound he got in Afghanistan.

I already know enough from med school that I could have helped. But I was only fourteen then. And nobody could make him go to doctors. He was stubborn that way.

He might not even approve of my med school, had he known. I like to think he'd be proud, though. No sense assuming any different.

I open the closet. It's empty. I realize there's not enough space for one of us, much less both, so I leave it to Nadia. Maybe she wants to discuss it before we fill it. It doesn't matter. I don't have much and no time to accumulate more.

There's a dresser up against the wall. I pull the drawers open. Also empty. I take only the bottom one. She can have the other two.

I don't need much in the drawer, just extra scrubs, socks, and underwear. I don't have a life outside of work at the moment. I remove my toiletry bag and leave my workout clothes and a few nicer outfits in the duffle.

I head to the kitchen. The cabinets are mostly empty

and the refrigerator bears only a stack of peach yogurt and a bag of apples. We will fill it in time.

Maybe I can spot a garage sale this weekend and nab some dishes. Mom loves a good yard sale. She copies the pickers on the TV shows and always offers a price for multiple things, so it seems like a lot of money even if she's getting half of it for free.

She's smart. Her ship simply never came in. I hope I can change that. I'm determined to. Now that I'm paying half of what I expected, I can send her more.

We were homeless more than once growing up, Dad going to one shelter, and Mom and I to another. If Dad was too bad off to leave, we would sleep in the backs of post offices that had all-night access to the mailboxes, mainly so we could all be together to make sure he was okay.

That won't happen again to Mom. Not on my watch.

I flip on the light in the bathroom. This smaller space smells of Nadia, a scent I didn't expect to already know.

My hair is wild and my eyes are bloodshot. That's terrifying.

I'm relieved to see there's a shower curtain up. I expected Nadia to do something pastel and feminine, but it's clear with cartoon images of cats all over it. Maybe she does rescue kittens.

I set my toiletry bag by the sink and return to the duffle to fetch one of my two towels plus something to sleep in.

Shower, then shut-eye.

The water is hot and plentiful, even if my cheap shampoo obliterates the smell of Nadia. I dry off and change into a T-shirt and shorts.

I consider my bag with a toothbrush and toiletries. I'll leave them in my zipper pouch for now. I shove it in the cabinet under the sink.

Nadia can have the shelves behind the mirror. She's bound to have more things than I do.

Right as I turn out the light, I sense a movement in the main room.

She can't be here. It's too early, plus there's no place that isn't obvious. There's only one big space plus the bathroom.

Still, I say, "Nadia?"

No answer.

It's dim in the main room with the lights out and the windows covered. I'm tired and probably seeing things. The place is unfamiliar.

The bed calls to me. I almost lie on it when I realize I shouldn't take over her pretty bedding.

I open the black trash bag that holds the old comforter I used on Jerry's floor for the last two weeks. It's black with the colorful figures of four Transformer figures emblazoned on both sides.

Jerry gave me real hell about it, but it's one of the few things I have from childhood. Mom would lug it around in a trash bag like this to make sure I was always warm and comfortable wherever we landed.

It's big enough to cover Nadia's ruffled number. As it lands over the expanse of the bed, I quickly follow its path.

I've just sunk my head against Optimus Prime when I sense another movement, a quick shadow near the floor.

Then a rustle of plastic.

I jump to my feet. A rat? This place seemed cleaner than that.

My ears tingle as I stand still to listen.

There's nothing.

But I can sense something here.

A broom leans against the wall. My fingers tighten around the handle. I sweep beneath the bed, instantly hitting several solid objects.

I flip on the flashlight function of my phone as a light and kneel to take a look. A row of suitcases fills the space, a matching set with Louis Vuitton stamped on the sides. Figures.

I scoot them with the broom, trying to flush out what's under there, not completely sure I want to deal with whatever it is.

Then something brushes against my forehead, soft and sweeping, like a feather. It's on the bed now.

I imagine a squirrel or a raccoon.

But I look up, and I swear it's a furry mountain lion staring down at me. It's huge. It opens its mouth, but no sound comes out.

Like a horror movie.

I back up like a crab, shocked and startled. The broom falls to the carpet with a thud.

But the thing doesn't move, tilting its head in a question.

What is it exactly?

It's a cat, but no cat like I've ever seen. It's the size of a cocker spaniel, with tan and black stripes like something wild.

"Who are you?" I ask.

It simply watches me.

"Are you friend or foe?"

It apparently decides I'm no threat and curls up on my transformer bedspread. It takes up a good quarter of the bed, its fuzzy tail wrapped elegantly around its body.

So it *is* a cat, maybe in its monster form.

I lift my phone to text Nadia about this intruder, then realize that I don't know her number. We never exchanged contact information even as we signed paperwork to share a home.

Is this cat hers? Is it one of her rescues? The one that made her ask about the pet policy at the first apartment?

She didn't mention it, but then we were always with the leasing agent when we were together.

It's one thing to hide an illegal cat when it's normal sized. But this one?

I reach out to poke it, but the monster feline narrows its gold eyes at me.

Yeah, it could probably eat me for breakfast.

I'm too long for the sofa, so I guess it's back to the floor for me, this time without so much as my Transformer blanket. At least there's carpet.

I might sleep with one eye open.

5

___

NADIA

The clock over the register reads ten. It's been a fast and furious morning prepping at the deli. Max took Camryn for a doctor's appointment, and I'm waiting on him to get back.

I need to leave the moment he arrives. Dalton will get off shift any minute, and I have to arrive at the apartment before he does.

"You got the cups?" Geneva asks, towering over me as I pull stacks from the stock below the soda fountain.

"I'm on it."

"Thanks." She heads to the kitchen.

I stand up to refill the cup rack.

Thank goodness Dalton works marathon shifts. When I got home from signing the lease and realized I didn't have his number, I knew I needed to catch him before he got to the studio for the first time.

I have to tell him about Cattarina the Great, also known as Catzilla.

It will take some doing to explain why I didn't

disclose her existence to the manager. And also cross my fingers that he's not allergic.

Because Max's wife Camryn is definitely allergic. Big time. She's been miserable since I moved in.

Catzilla sheds everywhere, and even though I keep her to my room, her hair has infiltrated every space in their cute house. Poor Camryn isn't allowed to take most allergy meds while she's pregnant, so she's had perpetually teary eyes and a red nose since I arrived a few weeks ago.

I was afraid if I told Dalton about her before signing the lease, he'd back out. I needed to plead her case away from the manager.

She's a total sweetheart and never causes any trouble or damage.

He'll love her. I know it.

The door jingles. I turn to see Max stride in.

Thank goodness.

"How's Max Junior?" I ask.

"He's a she!" he says.

I stand up. "Max! That's terrific!" I wrap my arms around his brawny frame. He's massive thanks to his bodybuilding hobby.

"Yeah, a little girl." He seems dazed.

"I can't wait to meet her," I say. "Did the appointment go well?"

"Sure, perfect. We had a sonogram." He flicks his phone to show a grainy black-and-white image.

I can't decipher any of it, but I say, "Beautiful! And Catzilla is out of the house, so she can breathe again!"

Max nods, pocketing his phone. "You sure you'll be all right living alone?"

I slug his arm, swallowing the lie. Max definitely can't know I'm rooming with a strange man. "Of course. I'm a big girl."

Vera comes out from behind the register. "Did I hear you're having a girl?"

"I am!"

Vera squeals, drawing several employees out of the kitchen. While they congratulate him, I untie my green and white apron and fold it. "Max, I have to run to the apartment. There are still some things to do."

"Go on. We've got this." He smiles over the handshakes and back slaps of his crew. I hurry to the back to grab my purse and dart out to my car.

I'll make sure Catzilla is happy and brushed. I'll clean out her litter box where it's hiding in a dark space under the bar. We'll both look adorable and charming, and surely Dalton won't make a fuss about her.

Maybe he's a cat lover?

I race the three miles to the new apartment, practicing my speech to the windshield. "Catzilla is the easiest pet imaginable. She can't meow due to a bronchial infection she had when she was rescued. So she won't make any noise!"

Of course, she's also gigantic. Maine Coons are big cats, and Catzilla is a stellar example of the breed. She looks more like a bobcat than a pet.

It will be okay. We'll be ready to woo Dalton.

But when I pull into our section of the complex, I

suck in a breath. Dalton's red Jeep is already in a slot. He got off early!

Oh, no. No, no!

I kill the car, pausing to rearrange my entire plea. "Dalton, she's my baby. I know you'll love her. Give her a chance."

We should have exchanged numbers. But we couldn't exactly do that in front of the apartment manager either. He thinks we're a couple!

What a terrible web of lies we're already trapped in!

As I walk to the door, I imagine the scenarios inside.

Maybe he's had a chance to adjust to Catzilla.

Maybe they're already in love!

It's also possible he hasn't seen her yet. Catzilla is extremely skittish with anyone but me, so if someone enters the room, she hides until she's comfortable.

Maybe she's been under the bed the whole time.

I draw in a steadying breath, then unlock the door.

It's dark inside, the blackout curtains drawn and the lights out. My rectangle of sunlight hits the floor in front of the sofa, and … what is that?

A head. Dalton's head is on the floor.

I rush inside. Is he okay?

He lies on his side on the beige carpet, his head resting on one arm. He's not in scrubs this time but baggy shorts and a blue T-shirt.

I drop to my knees next to him. "Dalton?" I shake his shoulder.

For a moment, he doesn't respond, and my heart lurches. "Dalton?" I say more urgently.

He rubs his eyes. "What's going on?"

Now I'm mad. I slug his shoulder. "What are you doing on the floor? I thought you were unconscious!"

"I was. What time is it?"

"Ten-fifteen. I thought I would beat you home."

"Aren't you supposed to be working at the deli?"

I stand up so that I tower over him. "I came to talk to you."

"About that?" He thumbs behind him, and in the shadowy gloom of the bed, I spot Catzilla on the pillow. She's pretending to be asleep, but I know better.

The jig is up. I close the front door and turn on the light.

Now Catzilla lifts her head. She opens her mouth, but of course there's no sound. It's a little eerie when she does that, but I'm used to it.

"Is that a Transformers bedspread?" I ask, turning back to Dalton.

He yawns. "Yes. And your cat, or whatever that thing is, took it from me. Have I only been asleep for thirty minutes?"

"I thought you wouldn't be here until eleven at the earliest."

"They turned us loose." He rubs his head, making his hair stand up. "I only have twelve hours off, though. I need to go back to sleep."

"On the Transformers bedspread?"

"Optimus Prime makes a good bedfellow." He lifts himself up onto the sofa. "I guess I could have tried to make this work." He lies down, his head on the armrest. He doesn't come close to fitting, his knees drawn up so his feet don't hang off. "Nope, that sucks." He sits up again.

I lift Catzilla off the bed. "I'm sorry I didn't tell you about Cattarina the Great ahead of time. I planned to tell you on the way to the car, but then you got caught up in a conversation with Evan."

"Cattarina? That's what you call her?"

"Catzilla for short."

"What is she?"

"A Maine Coon. She's big, I know, but she's very sweet and she can't meow. She's very neat—"

He waves me off. "It's fine."

"Fine? Really?" Could it be that easy?

"Sure."

I carry Cattarina over to the sofa and sit down. "Cat, this is Dalton. Don't be scared. He's very nice."

Cattarina is not convinced. She hunches down like she might leap off my lap at any moment.

I hold her firmly. "He's okay, Cattarina."

Slowly, she settles on my lap, her gold eyes fixed on Dalton.

He reaches out to pet her, but she springs unexpectedly from my lap, clears half the studio in the process, and skitters beneath the bed.

That didn't go well.

"She'll mostly hide," I say. "She's no trouble."

"It's fine. Look, I'm going to steal the bed while the stealing's good." He heads across the room to collapse on the Transformers. "I have another long shift tonight and tomorrow, then twenty-four off. We can talk then."

"Should we share contact information? That way I'll know your schedule and when not to wake you."

He reaches for his phone on the floor beside the bed. He unlocks it and tosses it across the room.

That's risky. I'm not athletic in the least. I fumble to catch it, but miss, of course. It bounces on the soft carpet.

I type my number into it and send myself a message so I get his.

By the time I've done that, he's asleep again. He was exhausted.

I tiptoe over to set the phone on the floor by the bed.

At least he knows about the kitty now.

I straighten, looking down on Dalton's form spread across the bed. He's muscular and tan, his hair flopping on his forehead.

I get the crazy urge to fix it, but I resist.

Roommates aren't for touching, even if they are cool with your secret oversized cat.

But the fact that I even thought about reaching for him is already worrisome.

6

———

DALTON

All six of us first-year interns are dead on our feet after a twenty-four-hour shift in the ER.

We barely murmur at each other, banging our lockers as we switch from doctor mode to humans.

Not that any of us feel human at the moment.

I might be slightly more perky than the others, despite the all-nighter. I am looking forward to my own apartment. My own bed.

Well, my own part-time bed.

Harrington drops onto a bench to switch his jacket and shoes like a medical version of Mr. Rogers, except he's a dead ringer for Chidi from *The Good Place*. It still works. "Where are you headed in such a hurry?"

I attempt to force my wild hair into some sort of order, then give up. "Settling into my new place."

"Finally free of sleeping on the floor?"

"Finally."

"Where'd you end up?"

"A small complex about three miles from here."

"Nice commute. I have to drive nearly an hour." Harrington stuffs his work shoes in a bag. "And now to go endure it. At least we have part of the weekend off."

"It's Friday?"

He laughs. "I know. Days become meaningless in here."

"They do."

Harrington claps my back. "Nice work with that kid who swallowed all the quarters. I thought we were going to have to sedate him to get an X-ray. You calmed him right down."

"I was a lot like him. I know what worked for me."

Harrington leads the way out of the locker room. "Swallowing money to hide it from your sister?"

"Nah, just doing dumb stuff and not wanting to admit it."

He grins. "You still do dumb stuff. I saw you ignoring that nurse in Trauma 4 who clearly wanted you to take an inventory of her bulbus vestibuli."

This makes me laugh. We all love a good clit joke. "Girlfriends aren't on the current agenda."

"I don't think she was asking for long-term status."

For some crazy reason Nadia pops into my head. "I have to get a handle on my life before I can drag a woman into it."

Harrington steps left to avoid an orderly rushing through the atrium at the front of the hospital. "Sounds like you're getting there. I would kill for a place that close."

"You might have to for the rent it costs."

As we push through the doors of the main entrance,

the air outside is fresh and cool. California nights. You can't beat them.

"See you next shift," Harrington says. He heads left for wherever he parked.

"Later." I turn right, aiming for Bernadette's red frame softly lit beneath a lamp. "You're a sight for sore eyes," I tell her, but for some reason the words conjure the image of Nadia.

Again. What the hell?

"Not going there," I mutter as I slide into the seat and fire up Bernadette's cranky engine.

I've got enough problems, and I can't add fantasizing about my roommate to the pile.

But when I pull up next to her Earl-blue Jeep, I realize, *uh oh*. We already have a schedule conflict.

It's evening. I'm home. She's home.

Who's getting the bed?

I'm tempted to knock on the door. Then I think, this is my place, too. If she wants to lounge around in her underwear, we'll both have to make peace with it.

But then I picture her in a lacy bra and panty set and suddenly, I need a minute. I can't go in there like a sex-starved creeper. Scrubs hide nothing.

I sigh and take off for the courtyard.

Nobody's at the pool. I park on a chair and think about our predicament.

I hadn't planned past the first few nights when we took the place. Of course some of my shifts are going to end when she's home.

Shit.

I tug my phone out of my pocket to text her.

Me: Hey, I'm getting off shift and realize we'll both be here.
Nadia: I already figured out we'd be off at the same time.
Me: I saw you were home.
Nadia: Where are you?
Me: By the pool.
Nadia: Night swimming?
Me: Thinking.
Nadia: I made a lasagna. You're welcome to some when you are done with your deep poolside thoughts.

She made dinner? To share?

My stomach growls at the mere thought of it.

Me: Coming.

I wait a moment to see if she'll text anything back, but when she doesn't, I head to the gate.

When I open the door to the apartment, she's sitting at the bar. I glance around, looking for the cat, but the oversized furball must be hiding again. I haven't seen her since Nadia introduced her.

She's dressed a lot like the day she found me on the floor. Jeans. T-shirt. Her pink socks have the words "I'm just a girl who loves" on one foot, but the other one is tucked beneath her on the stool. Now I'm dying to know what it says. Wine? Cheese? Sex?

There I go again.

I drop my keys and badge on the dresser. A few of her things are already there. Her phone on a charger. A small wooden box. A bottle of hand lotion with flowers on it. I wonder if it's the source of how she smells.

Focus, Dalton.

I head over to the bar. Nadia is in front of an empty plate, a few traces of red sauce on its surface. Her fork is lying neatly across it, like she finished a formal meal and is indicating to the waitstaff that they can take her plate.

She holds a book open, but I can't quite make out the text. She closes it, cover down. The back is pink. She rests her arm over it like she's trying to hide it.

Interesting.

"I picked up a few dishes," she says. "Some plates, a bit of silverware, and a baking pan or two. My sister-in-law Camryn gave me a few pots she never uses. It's not much, but we can get by for a while."

"Sounds good." I move past the bar and into the kitchen. I open a few cabinets, locating the short stack of plates and pulling one down. There are also four plastic glasses on the shelf. I take one of those as well and fill it with tap water.

"I'll pick up some groceries during this break I have," I tell her. "Should we designate sections of the fridge, or will we know whose is whose?"

"I'll take the right side," she says. "I often bring things home from the deli. We can make that communal food, because I have more than I can eat, anyway."

That's a perk. "Awesome. And thank you for sharing your lasagna. I am starved."

"I figured you would be. Are all your shifts twenty hours or more?"

"Not always."

We obviously don't have a spatula, because a fork and a butter knife sit inside the dish to serve the lasagna. I cut off a hefty piece. "Sometimes I do twelve on, twelve off. It's only my third week, so it's not clear to me yet how it will work."

She nods. "My schedule is mostly set. Tuesday through Friday, eight a.m. to four, and alternating Saturday or Sunday. But sometimes I cover for my cousin and work more."

I've inhaled three bites while she said that, but I swallow to ask, "You work with your cousin?"

"For him. Sort of. He owns the deli. I'm helping while he has so much on his plate with a baby coming. They found out they're having a girl."

I swallow again, finally slowing down enough to actually taste it. It's good, creamy and tangy, with layers of pasta on a pillow of ricotta. "That's nice. And this is delicious."

"Thanks. I have a few things I can cook."

"And I guess you're a master at sandwiches."

She laughs. "Not what I expected to be doing at this point, but I'm not sure what my next step is."

"I'm sure you'll figure it out." I try to slow how fast I'm eating. It's good.

She tries to shove her book away with her elbow, but I catch her.

"Watcha reading?"

Her cheeks pink up, and I wonder what else on her body might have a similar vasodilation. Breasts? Thighs?

There I go again.

"Nothing," she says.

I slide the fork through my lasagna. "You're embarrassed by it?"

"No!" But she picks up the book and spins off the stool before I can see it.

"You are!"

"It's … private."

"I like a good erotic novel myself."

She halts on her way to the dresser. "It's not erotic!" Then she hesitates. "I mean, depending on what you consider erotic. It has … scenes in it."

"Erotic scenes?"

"Oh, you!"

I swivel on the stool to face her. "Let me see it!"

"Fine." She tosses the book to me. It thuds into my stomach, but I catch it.

I turn it over and read the title aloud. "*First Base to Love.*" I flip through the pages until I spot the word "cock." I pause, reading a few lines, then snap it closed. This will not help cool my jets.

Nadia lunges for the book. "What did you find?" She flips through it, like she could locate what I saw.

"Just something about a *throbbing cock*. That doesn't sound like *first* base."

Her face flames so red I wonder if she should lie down and elevate her legs. "It's a baseball romance."

"So he hits a home run?"

Something akin to a growl forms in her chest. "I knew this was a bad idea."

I hold up my hands. "I'm all for a good sexy read! Don't worry about it."

She moves as far from me as possible, sitting on the corner of the bed. It's back in blue ruffle mode, my Transformer bedspread neatly rolled up by the wall.

I scrape together the dregs of my lasagna and swallow. Dang, that's good. But I'm headed toward a wall of exhaustion. I can feel it.

Still, I should try to smooth things over. "It's fine. You're going to find out things about me. I'm going to learn stuff about you. We're adults. It will be okay."

She flips through the pages, her cheeks pink. "Okay."

"Maybe we can do a book club."

She lifts the book in the air like she might chuck it at me again.

"No need for violence! I'll do the dishes." I head into the kitchen, picking up both of our plates from the bar.

"I'll help."

"No, you cooked. I can clean."

I watch her from the corner of my eye as I scrub the cheese off our plates and set them in the dishwasher.

When I've put away the leftover lasagna and cleared the bar, I notice she's back to reading the book, this time without hiding the cover.

That's better.

7

NADIA

I lean against the wall, my feet pulled up onto the bedspread and my arms around my knees, as Dalton cleans up dinner.

It's good to know he's willing to help. I had imagined doing everything for a messy, overworked man playing the doctor card.

But he seems perfectly at home at the sink and knows how to load the rack in the dishwasher.

Our exchange about the romance novel was … interesting.

I have an entire suitcase of them below the bed. I know Dalton won't go looking for them. I can already tell he's not a snooper.

But I'm not going to set them out even though there's a cute set of shelves over the end of the bar.

I'm not embarrassed by my book collection, although the word cock might appear slightly more than, say, inside *War and Peace*. But I barely know Dalton, and I'd prefer to dole out information about me in a controlled manner.

And yet, learning that I can't stop reading *First Base to Love* even knowing full well Dalton was on his way to the apartment, might be an essential fact. I thought for sure I could make it to the end of the chapter before he walked in from the pool.

I hadn't thought he'd be so interested. The Dalton I've known so far has mainly been … well, *tired*.

Which brings us to the next problem.

Who is going to get the bed?

My knees protest my position, so I straighten my legs right as Dalton sets down the dish towel on the bar and sits on the sofa.

We face each other across the large room.

He stares at my feet. "I was wondering what those said."

"What said?"

"Your socks."

"Oh." I self-consciously pull in my feet to sit cross-legged.

"So, you love *pickles*?" He says it the way he'd said "cock" earlier.

Oh, God, he thinks it means penis. Like the eggplant emoji does on social media.

"Pickles, like the deli. My family is *really* into pickle jokes."

He leans back, elbows out, his hands clasped behind his head. In his scrubs, his biceps bulging above the sleeves, he could be filming an episode of *Grey's Anatomy*.

Which I've watched. Three times through.

Is he a Dr. McDreamy? Or more of a Dr. McHottie?

I have to shake this line of thinking off. *All the way* off.

But it's hard to shed that initial attraction we had in the courtyard. Especially when we're this close, this informal, this *cozy*.

"So tell me one," he says.

I've gone so far out in my train of thought that I have to go back and find the thread of conversation. "A pickle joke?"

"Sure, if your family has so many."

"No."

"No?"

"I'm not a good joke teller."

His grin sends my heart skittering. "But I'm an excellent audience. I promise to laugh like you're Taylor Tomlinson."

"You like her?" She's my favorite comedian.

"Love her. See, we have something in common." He yawns and quickly covers his mouth.

"You have to be exhausted. You haven't slept since yesterday."

"Nope, I'm wide awake and ready for a pickle joke."

He's not going to drop it.

"Okay, but only one."

"Excellent." He kicks off his shoes and crosses one foot over his ankle.

"Okay, let me think." I run through the repertoire Uncle Sherman loves to pull out at Christmas. Max is also one to repeat the favorites.

There's the dill dough one. No, not going there.

The giggling dills. No. Not funny enough.

The door being a-jar. No. I hate that one.

His voice jolts me out of my concentration. "You're overthinking."

"I'm not."

"You are." There's that grin again. "Say the next one that comes to mind."

"I can't—"

"Come on."

"Oh, okay. What's the difference between a pickle and a therapist?"

The minute I start it, I'm swamped with regret. Not that one! Why did I say the worst one of all?

I wrack my brains to come up with a punch line that isn't the real one.

"I don't know," Dalton says.

"Try," I tell him, hoping to stall. I have to think of something. Pickles don't have sofas? Pickles don't charge by the hour? Oh, God!

"I really don't know," he says. "You've got me. What is the difference between a pickle and a therapist?"

I have to go through with it. I make it as deadpan as possible so he won't think I purposefully brought up male anatomy again.

"If you don't know the difference, stop talking to your pickle."

He hesitates a moment, then laughs so hard and so long, I wonder if he's gotten punchy from being tired.

"You got me," he says. "Good one."

I scoot off the bed. "I think you need to sleep." I

drag my blue comforter off the top so that he can use his.

"I didn't think we'd have a conflict so soon."

"We should have known there would be days off that lined up." I fold up the bulky fabric and set it on the end of the sofa opposite from where he sits.

"I'm not taking your bed." His voice is firm.

"I'm not taking it from a doctor working twenty-four-hour shifts!" I give him what I hope is a stern expression.

But when I get a good look, I can see the exhaustion that he's hiding. It's in the creases around his eyes, the way he pushes his hair off his forehead.

I have to do something. "Besides," I say airily. "I'm about to go out. It's a Friday night, and I'm meeting girlfriends."

"Oh?" This surprises him.

"Yes, we get all dressed up and hit the clubs."

"At this hour?" It is almost nine.

"Nothing good happens before ten." That used to be true when I was twenty-two. But during the rigors of grad school, I gave up my late nights.

His eyebrows knit together. "All right then."

"I need to get an outfit and change. Then I'll be out of your hair so you can sleep all you want."

"Okay."

I kneel by the bed and pull out the mid-sized bag. "Have we figured out the closet situation?" I ask. "I saw you took the bottom drawer of the dressers."

"You can have the closet. I don't need much space."

"Okay." I unzip the bag and pull out the first dress I

see, a shimmery black number I wore to a charity ball with my brother Axel. He's always going to those things.

Dalton's eyes go wide. "That's what you wear to clubs?"

"It's LA." I try to say it with conviction, as if I haven't spent every weekend since I got here in my room at Max's house with Catzilla. Speaking of which, where is she?

I lean down and peer under the bed again. After a moment, I make out the glint in her eyes. "Oh, sweet kitty," I say. "You can come out."

"I feel bad that she's scared of me."

"She'll adjust, eventually. She started warming up to Max after a week or so." I tap the floor, but Catzilla only watches me from her corner.

"Maybe I can bribe her to come out. What does she like? Tuna? Milk?"

"Catzilla isn't motivated by food. Never has been."

"Then she hasn't had your lasagna."

Huh, another compliment. I return to the suitcase, drag out a pair of black heels, then close it up and roll the whole thing into the closet. It barely fits.

"You can have the mirror cabinet in the bathroom, too," Dalton says with another yawn. "I'll keep things in my bag."

"You sure?"

He nods, and his eyes blink longer and longer.

Maybe if he falls asleep, I won't have to keep up the ruse that I'm going out.

But he pulls out his phone. "You have fun."

I head into the bathroom. I'm not sure where I will

go all gussied up. Definitely not to Max's. He'll ask too many questions, and I'll crack.

I guess I could get coffee at a diner. And read. There are more books in my Jeep.

I change into the dress and turn to the mirror. My messy bun and lack of makeup do not match whatsoever. I guess I'll do the whole thing.

I quickly add a smoky eye and hurried contour. I let my hair down, brushing it out. I don't want to take time to curl it. Besides, it practically cries out in pain when I try to take it out of its iron-straight default mode.

I part it down the middle and let it fall in a long, loose cascade. With the dramatic eye, it works.

The shoes add four inches to my height. I smooth the fitted dress over my hips. Is this what it's going to be like whenever Dalton and I have a bed conflict?

I'll figure it out. That's something I can do at the diner. Determine if we can fit a hideaway bed somewhere, just for nights like this. Maybe if we leave the closet empty, it can be stowed in there.

I open the door quietly, half expecting him to be asleep already.

But he's tapping on his phone.

"I'm heading out," I say.

When he looks up, his whole body goes still. I recognize the interest in his eyes. He's seeing me the same way he did when we met.

He swallows hard. "Oh, hey, yeah. You clean up."

"It can't be all deli shirts and jeans." I fidget with my dress, not sure I can handle him looking at me the way he is. It's like he's a wolf, and I'm a little white rabbit frozen in the grass.

"Will you be out all night?" he asks.

He thinks I'm going to hook up with someone. Should I let him think it?

I evade. "Get some rest." I hurry across the room to snatch up my purse. It's a brown sack of a thing, completely wrong for the outfit, but it doesn't matter. I have to get out of here, away from his hungry gaze and borderline jealousy of my nonexistent hookup.

He stands. "Call me if you need backup. Or security. Or something."

I throw open the door. "I'm a big girl!"

Then I'm outside. Only when I'm halfway to my car do I breathe again.

I shouldn't be surprised that we're already veering out of roommates territory. We did have that moment before we figured out we were rivals.

And now we're not. We live together. Meals. Showers. Bed times.

Nights.

I sit in my Jeep a moment, willing my heart to calm down.

This apartment situation is going to be more than I bargained for.

8

DALTON

I don't intend to crash before showering, but I make the mistake of sitting on the Transformer bedspread after Nadia leaves.

Then I'm keeling over, apparently the last of my energy used up on digesting perfect pasta and sparring with my roommate over verbal innuendos.

When I wake up around four a.m., Nadia's not here. The kitchen light is on.

And the cat is watching me from the sofa.

I lift my head. "Hello, Catzilla."

She opens her mouth in a silent response.

"Still spooky."

I sit up slowly, trying to avoid startling her into running. She can't get to her preferred hiding place without coming closer.

I should go back to sleep.

But where is Nadia? Did she stay over with some guy?

The mere thought of it banishes all thought of sleep. Her fancy dress on the floor. Her hair all mussed.

No, no. Think of something else.

I ease off the bed. My bladder requires attention, and I might as well shower.

My socks are silent on the carpet, and I hug the wall to show the cat that I'm not coming for her.

She turns to watch me as I move, coiled tightly in her spot, ready to spring. As soon as I've cleared the path between the sofa and the bed, she darts across the room in two long leaps and disappears into the darkness between the suitcases.

"I'm an all-right guy, I promise!"

It's pointless, at least for now. I realize I've forgotten to get a clean set of clothes, but I don't want to disturb the cat even more. I'll grab something when I'm done. She should have at least a moment's peace.

Nadia's things have spread through the space. Makeup on the counter. More bottles on the corners of the bathtub. I pull my toiletry bag out from beneath the sink and start the water.

I'll need to figure out where the laundry room is. This longer break is my time to wash everything.

I discard my clothes on a white rug that wasn't there yesterday. Living with a woman is nice. The shower is as hot and hearty as I remember, and I let out a long groan as the heat penetrates my shoulders and back.

I haven't had a moment to take in where I'm at. It's been a whirlwind, getting Mom situated back in North Carolina, driving to LA, dealing with my first weeks at

South General and crashing at Jerry's. Then the apartment hunt, and here we are.

Nadia Armstrong. She is something, with her flashing eyes and quick temper. I remember how she acted that first day.

But then there are the romance novels and her rescue cat. She was embarrassed to be caught reading or even tell a joke about dicks.

Speaking of which, mine is twitching just thinking about her.

Nope. Nope. Self-correct. The last thing Nadia needs is her roommate getting off in the shower to the image of her … sliding off that sexy dress, revealing a black bra and panties. Her skin glowing, breasts testing the limits of the lacy cups.

She wears the heels, and long legs with dimples at the knees lead to that triangle of satin I want to remove with my teeth.

Fuck. Too late. I've gone rigid and there's no point denying the direction my mind is going. I try to switch to some other woman. I settle on a blond nurse who often comes down when we transfer a patient to that wing.

But it won't stick, and by the time I'm pulsing into my hand, Nadia is back, a vision of her in the shower with me. Her long dark hair is wet in the flow of water, streams of it flowing down her body.

Fuuuuuuuck. I scrub myself down again.

This is not a direction I need to be going. But if I can't control my thoughts, I sure as hell better take charge of how I act around her. Because she can't know the stranger she's been around for less than a week is already picturing her naked.

I turn off the water and snatch up my towel. It's hanging next to Nadia's, mine a gray battered rag compared to her pretty pink one.

Opposites. I have to remember that. Regardless of whatever led her to need to share a cheap furnished apartment with a man she barely knows, she comes from means. Recent ones. Her clothes are nice. Her accessories, too. Louis Vuitton luggage and Coach bags.

As I rub my head with the towel, I'm wildly curious about her circumstances. She knows everything about mine.

I hang the towel back on the bar, careful that my damp one doesn't touch hers. I reach for my clean clothes when I remember I didn't bring any inside. I was trying to be kind to the cat.

I'll have to disturb her. I shove the dirty clothes into the laundry bag I hung on the back of the door and head out into the living room to retrieve my duffle.

The air conditioner is on full blast and it feels amazing against my damp skin.

Then I hear a sharp gasp.

It's Nadia, back from her walk of shame, still in the shiny dress, holding her heels in one hand.

And I'm buck naked.

9

NADIA

O h. My. God.

Seeing Dalton tricked out in scrubs is one thing, and asleep in a T-shirt and shorts is another.

But currently, my roommate is standing outside of the bathroom without a stitch on.

The light from behind him halos his damp hair and leaves shadows that define every muscle. His shoulders are broad and carved like marble. His chest is honed and hairless, like an underwear model.

But there's no underwear to model here. The long plane of his belly slides directly into a V that points right at a part of his anatomy that must know I'm looking. It starts to take shape, lifting and growing like it has a life of its own.

I can't stop staring.

"Shit," Dalton says, and the object of my intense stare is turned from my view, leaving me with a wide back and butt cheeks that ought to be put on posters.

He darts back into the bathroom. "I didn't know you were here!" he calls out. "Shit! I'm sorry!"

I'm not. I feel thunderstruck, pinned to the carpet until the view returns.

But when it does, he's wrapped himself in a towel. I'm missing the midsection, but I get the full effect of his chest and arms and legs.

"I didn't grab my clothes. Your cat … I didn't want to disturb her. I didn't know. I—" He stammers on, but I manage to tear my gaze from his body and set my bag on the sofa.

"I wasn't sure you'd be up yet," I say, tucking a hunk of hair behind my ear.

"I am. I crashed. I should have planned better."

"It's fine."

He rushes over to the bed and kneels down to drag out an army duffle. He's so busy tunneling through his clothes that he doesn't notice when the towel gets loose and falls off.

I sit on the sofa, trying to stifle my giggle. There's that glorious butt again, perched on strong calves as he squats and searches for an outfit.

He stands abruptly, then realizes he's lost the towel again.

"For Christ's sake," he says, bending down to snatch it, giving me an incredible view of the back of his thighs.

When does he get a chance to work out? Maybe he had more free time before his internship.

Then he's covered again.

I bite my lip to force my smile down before he turns around.

He heads back to the bathroom. "I'll be back. Decent this time." The door slams shut.

I take the moment to pull a pair of sleep shorts and an oversized T-shirt from a drawer. I'm not sure what he's going to be up to next, but I'm dead on my feet. Thankfully, I don't work tomorrow. My weekend shift is Sunday.

His Transformer bedspread is rumpled. I realize we're sharing a pillow. I sit on the bed and lean down to sniff it.

It smells mostly of me, my hair products and a whiff of floral shampoo. But mixed in there is something that is definitely Dalton.

He steps out and I quickly sit up.

"I didn't expect you back at this hour," he says, trying to casually lean on his elbow on the surface of the bar, missing, then shifting in place to try again.

He's rattled.

"I went to an all-night diner," I tell him. That part's true. I stayed there for seven straight hours, finished my book, and ate three pieces of pie with six cups of coffee.

"Oh. I thought…" He trails off.

"You thought what?"

"Nothing. I have dumb thoughts."

I pick up my sleeping clothes. I'm halfway to the bathroom when it hits me. "You thought I hooked up with some guy and was at his place?"

He won't meet my gaze.

I guess I shouldn't argue the point. Let him think

what he wants. It's not like I *wouldn't* have a one-nighter. It's just that typically, I don't. I'm cautious. And LA is known for its sharks.

"I guess I didn't realize you had a lot of friends here," he said. "Since you said you were new to town, like me."

Oh, this lie is going to bite me on the butt. I almost say they are work friends from the deli, but given the cast of characters involved, only one of whom fits the might-go-to-the-club demographic, I'm too likely to get caught later.

Better to say nothing. I move into the bathroom and close the door.

It's steamy from Dalton's shower. I breathe in the warm air and the smell of his herbal bath wash.

His bottles rest on the edge of the tub. I take a moment to rearrange mine so there is room for his.

The mirror is obscured, so I wipe it down with my towel. I notice his laundry bag hanging on the back of the door.

It's not my space but both of ours. It might be small, but we'll have to figure things out.

Like sleeping.

I remove all the makeup and twist my hair into a quick bun. By the time I'm ready for bed, it's almost six a.m. and I'm exhausted. I'm the one who's been up for twenty-four hours now.

But I have nothing to do today. And we have blackout curtains, something I picked up immediately, knowing Dalton would be sleeping at odd hours.

When I come out, he's sitting on the sofa. He looks

up, and the heat of his gaze touches my legs, face, and the shirt where my braless nipples are poking the fabric.

I feel almost as naked as he was, but the way heat pools in me tells me my reaction is almost as strong as his was earlier when I saw him. His was just more obvious.

This is a problem. It's one thing to room with a stranger. It's another thing entirely to feel an attraction to him.

I have to knock it off.

"I'm pretty tired," I tell him.

"I have errands," he says. "And I want to go for a run before it gets hot."

I drag my blue comforter over to the bed. He's already removed his Transformer blanket. "Do you always shower before you run?"

He doesn't answer, and I wonder if I've caught *him* in a white lie.

This will never do.

I toss my bedding onto the mattress. "Look," I say.

"Hey," he says at the same moment.

We both laugh a little.

"You first," he says.

I sit on the bed. "I think we need to accept that there will be occasional awkwardness."

"Agreed," he says.

"But we also need to be honest about things."

He frowns. "Okay."

"You don't have to make up some excuse to get out of my way. And I won't make up any to get out of yours." I look up at the ceiling. "Maybe we can string up some sort of curtain so we can both be here when one of us is sleeping."

"That's a good idea."

"And we should agree that we shouldn't put ourselves out to avoid the other one. We have to co-exist here."

"Agreed."

"So don't feel like you need to go anywhere," I tell him.

"But, I really do plan to go for a run," he says.

I lie down and pull the blue comforter over me. "Okay, Dalton."

"I'll be back after lunch. And I'll get my own pillow. And see if I can spot some curtainy thing."

"That'll be good."

"You want me to put your cell on the charger?" He picks up the phone I left on the sofa.

"That would be nice."

He crosses the room and plugs it in on the dresser. "Sweet dreams."

I'm not sure he says anything else, because I am out cold.

10

DALTON

The next few shifts work out like Nadia and I planned. I get in early in the morning, either after Nadia is gone or with only an hour of crossover.

When she isn't there, I sleep or organize a few things. We get a small nightstand with two drawers. A curtain to divide the room. More dishes. The fridge slowly fills with groceries, condiments, and leftovers.

She makes big casseroles and leaves notes for what I can eat.

I buy extra pizza or pasta or a second burger and leave some for her.

It's working.

But about two weeks into our roommate situation, I get two whole days off, starting in the evening.

Our sleep schedules are going to align twice.

When I enter the apartment, Nadia is cooking. The amazing smell of garlic fills the air.

"Please tell me you're making extra," I say, dropping onto the sofa.

"Totally. I wouldn't leave you out."

I kick back, leaning my head on the arm, watching her move around the kitchen. She's wearing a deli shirt and khakis. Her dark hair is braided down her back. It's soothing to watch her stir a pot, shift to a cutting board, and slice an onion.

I wonder who else has gotten to see her like this. "Have you had many roommates before?"

She scoots the onion into the pan. A new, wonderful aroma fills the apartment. "I have. I lived with my friend Sheila throughout grad school."

Wait, what? I sit up abruptly. "Grad school? You have a Master's? Or a Ph.D.?"

"An MBA." She doesn't break stride, cutting a stick of butter into chunks.

I head for the bar and perch on a stool. "Why are you making deli sandwiches, then?" This could be the answer to everything I've been wondering about her.

"Stalling."

The butter goes into the microwave and she punches buttons before facing me. "My family expects me to work for Pickle Media, and I'm not sure I want to."

"So you're a rebel."

"A rebel in plastic food service gloves." The microwave dings, and she pulls out the melted butter, peering into the bowl. "I enjoy cooking. I don't mind slicing and dicing all day. Not a fan of customer service. People can be so rude."

"Tell me about it. Wait until they come into the ER and get mad at you because you have to pull glass out of their butt."

Nadia freezes, a cup of measured flour tilted over the bowl of butter. "Glass? In their butt?"

"You'd be amazed at how often people who've made the dumbest mistakes get nasty with you for trying to fix it."

She continues with her recipe, adding various spices to the flour and butter. I haven't teased out what she's making yet.

"That's just wrong. Doctors should be revered. You're saying that's changed?"

"I think it changed a long time ago."

She stirs, her head tilted. "What do you think caused it?"

"Insurance. Cost of care. We're mixed up in it even though we don't like it any more than they do."

"But in the hospital, you don't have anything to do with billing or approvals, do you?"

I shift on the stool. "You'd be surprised at how many people ask how much this will cost way before how long it will take to get better."

"I believe it."

She leans over the warm stove to stir the garlic and onions. The tendrils at her temple curl in the heat. Her features are elegant with a sharp nose, defined jaw, long lashes. She looks like a fifties model, Elizabeth Taylor maybe.

"How long do you think you have before your family will try to force your hand?" I ask.

She shrugs as she opens a carton of chicken broth. "I signed a lease to make it harder for them to call me back to New York or Florida."

"Those are the options?"

"If I'm going to be upper management, yes. We have delis in Boulder, where I'm from, as well as Texas and here, of course. But the restaurants aren't the point anymore. We have entire enterprises around advertising, marketing, and product development."

"Who's in charge of it all?"

"Uncle Sherman, although if you ask him, he'll insist he's retired. He turned over the main deli in Manhattan to my cousin Anthony a few years ago."

"Isn't he the one who went viral after poisoning that TV chef?"

"Yeah, that was something."

"You Pickles are kind of a big *dill*."

"Ha, ha." She pours the broth into a big pot, moving it on the burner that held the pan with the garlic.

I stand up to be nearer to the amazing smells. "What are you making?"

"Dumplings."

"It smells like heaven."

"We had a lot of leftover chicken at the deli, so I brought it to dump in. Can you get it from the fridge? It's wrapped in white paper."

It's nice working with her in the kitchen. I open the door and retrieve the oblong package.

"Thanks." She opens it and chunks of chicken plop into the broth.

"Since you like to cook, did you want your own restaurant in the chain?"

She shakes her head. "Nope. That would take my happy hobby into work territory."

I lean against the counter. "What did you imagine doing with your MBA?"

She adds the onions and garlic to the dough. "I think I was on auto-pilot. My two oldest brothers got MBAs."

"Do they work for Pickle Media?"

"Rhett works for Dougherty, the Florida outpost."

"How many brothers do you have?"

"Three."

"Did the other two escape?"

She sets down her spoon. "Axel sold his hiking app during college, and he's all set. He got, like, half a billion."

I nearly choke on my own spit. "Half a billion?"

"Yeah. It was a good app. He's really into the outdoors."

"I bet. And the other one?"

"He's gone domestic." She turns around at that. "What about your family?"

This might bring down the conversation. I keep it light. "It's just me and my mom. She lives in North Carolina. She works at Wal-mart right now. She doesn't hold down a job for long, though. She has zero tolerance for bullshit."

"And your dad? Or is that too personal?"

And there it is. "He died when I was fourteen. Complications from a war injury."

"Oh!" She presses her hand to her chest, like

learning this about me pains her. "Is that his army duffle under the bed?"

"Yeah."

Her eyebrows knit together. "I can't imagine losing my dad, although my Aunt Pat died when I was a kid. I always worried about my cousins. Anthony, the youngest, was only sixteen."

"It's rough being a teenager when it happens." And homeless, to boot, but I don't say that. Dad got to die in a clean, white bed in the hospital. "But we got by."

She flashes a smile. "I bet you did. You seem resourceful. When did you know you wanted to be a doctor?"

That is too tough of a story for this night, so I fake my answer. "When I figured out how much money they made."

"Not saving human lives?"

I shrug. One life, mainly, but I was too young. "I will be a perfect philanthropist."

"I'm well-versed in charity balls."

"When I go to my first one, I'll be sure to call on you to coach me."

She stirs the broth and chicken. "They aren't all they're cracked up to be. Neither is money."

"Only people with money say that."

She spoons a lump of dough into the boiling water. "Fair enough."

"Any noise from the family about you staying here in LA?"

"Not yet. As long as I'm helping Max and Cam, they won't question it."

"When is she due?"

"Four months."

"And then?"

She plops more dough into the pot. "I'm helping them while they have a newborn."

"How long do you figure you can stretch this?"

"I have a year lease. Max hasn't spilled that I've moved yet, and I'm not telling anyone. But they'll figure it out, eventually."

"And you have no plan."

She scrapes the bottom of the dough bowl. "I'm tired of plans. I want to go without one for a while."

Her voice is laced with frustration. I'm starting to understand her, little by little. She had expectations thrust onto her. She's not sure how to get out from under them.

I had nobody expecting me to amount to much of anything, not even Mom, who suggested I join her at the fast-food restaurant she was working at when I turned sixteen.

But I started studying for my SAT instead. I knew my grades were bad, but I somehow qualified to be a National Merit Scholar with my PSAT. It was the first jolt of success that told me that maybe I was smarter than I looked. That I had potential.

As I watch Nadia cover the pot and wash out the bowl, I can't imagine the opposite scenario. That everyone tells you what you ought to be, makes you aim high. But when you get there, it's all wrong.

Nadia must spot her cat because she says, "Come here, baby girl." She sits on the sofa and pats the seat.

I hold still, watching the oversized cat slowly step out from where she's peeking between suitcases. It's a rare sighting for me. She mostly hides under the bed.

"Come on," Nadia says.

Catzilla crosses the room, her gaze trained on me. I barely breathe, trying to avoid startling her.

She leaps silently onto the sofa.

"Good girl," Nadia says. "My sweet baby." She strokes the cat's long fur.

"Do you miss rescuing kittens?" I ask, keeping my voice low.

"Sometimes. But once I got Cattarina, I had to stop anyway. She loved the kittens, but they were terrified of her."

"I imagine."

"Did you have pets growing up?" she asks.

I picture the places we lived, the shelters, the hovels, the single rooms in dingy houses. "No."

"Did you want one?"

"Sure. I wanted a dog like most kids."

"Catzilla loves dogs, if they're not afraid of her. You could get one."

I grin at her. "One secret pet might be enough civil disobedience for us."

Nadia presses her cheek against Catzilla's head. "I guess I should tell them I have her. With you paying half the rent, I can probably afford the fees."

"You're not half the rebel I thought you were."

"You thought I was a rebel?"

"The way you fought for that first apartment? You were fierce! You accused me of wearing fake scrubs."

Her cheeks go pink. "I'm sorry about that. I was feeling desperate."

"So was I. But look at how this is working out."

She nods, petting the cat's head. "It is, isn't it?"

And the contentment in that moment, a roof over my head, warm dumplings filling the space with savory smells, and this woman with her cat, makes me realize I missed out on a lot growing up half-homeless.

And I like it. Here. With her.

A lot.

11

NADIA

I can't believe how well things are working out with Dalton.

With the curtain creating a bedroom, we manage more privacy. We get a blow-up mattress for the nights we're both there. He happily takes it when there's a conflict, even though every time, I try to convince him to alternate.

Catzilla won't approach him, even as time stretches to a month together, but she will be in the same room with him without bolting.

It's progress.

We don't have any other repeats of his naked apartment walk, and while there is an undercurrent between us since then, it doesn't seem to affect anything.

He might be the perfect roommate.

On a Friday in early August, Max and Camryn invite me to a gathering at a dive bar in East LA near the gym where Max works out. They think I'm not meeting people, always either working at the deli or holed up in my apartment alone.

They still don't know about Dalton.

Camryn warns me to dress down for Aces, which has a rough crowd, but their friends like it.

It's the first time I've been out on a weekend night in LA. Max and Cam's friends are all mixed martial arts fighters, trainers, and promoters. She used to do professional tans for their competitions until she got pregnant and wanted to limit the chemicals.

I wear an artfully ripped pair of jeans that shows my knees, and a white tank top beneath a thin red cardigan that falls off one shoulder. It's cute, but not fancy or attention-grabbing, especially paired with red Converse.

I lowball the jewelry, just a stack of red bracelets and a gold chain. I leave my hair straight and long, like I didn't bother with it even though I painstakingly roller brushed it smooth with the hair dryer.

Dalton isn't around when I leave. His shift will end between ten and midnight. I let him know I won't be home until late, off with my cousins.

Since we'll both be home tonight, the air mattress is already set out, although not blown up yet, as we never know if Catzilla might dig her claws into it while we're gone.

I don't take my car. Max suggested I grab a ride to the bar, since parking is terrible, and it's not exactly the safest place, anyway. He's not risking his.

Is it that bad? I peer out the window of the Uber at the blocks of small businesses lined up in long, low buildings. Laundromats. Vape shops. Coffee. Tiny restaurants with the windows covered.

It's definitely not Rodeo Drive.

But the people look the same as anywhere, sitting at bus stops, talking in groups on corners. Cyclists zoom by, ignoring the red light.

"You sure you want to go to a bar down here alone?" The woman behind the wheel taps her phone while we're stopped.

"I'm meeting four MMA fighters, a bodybuilder, and their friends. I'll be all right."

"Oh yeah, MMA is a big scene down here." She turns to peer at me. "You happen to know Colt McClure? He's my favorite."

"I don't, but I think my cousin Max does."

"If you see him, you tell him Valerie Corellli thinks he's great."

I bite back a smile. "Will do."

The light turns green and we dart forward.

"That's where he used to train," Valerie says, pointing at the darkened windows of a place called Buster's Gym. "They used to have this big ol' banner over it with his picture. I loved those days."

"My cousin works out there."

"Who's your cousin?"

"Max Pickle."

"Oh, I know him! He's not a fighter. He does those muscle competitions. Now he's a looker. He single? I'm single."

"He and his wife Cam are having a baby soon."

"Well, rats. The good ones are always taken." She

signals and pulls over to the curb. There are two metal doors in the long brick wall, no windows. "This is the bar. Make sure they're here before you go in there. I don't want to drop you off alone."

I text Max. *You here? I just pulled up.*

After a moment, Max steps out of one of the doors and waves a hand.

"Oh, you weren't lying! That's him!" Valerie practically lies forward on the front seat to peer out the passenger-side window.

"Thank you for the ride." I close the app and open the door.

Max rushes forward to help me out.

"Hi, Max Pickle!" Valerie calls. "Tell your friend Colt McClure that he's the greatest!"

Max leans down. "Who should I say thinks he's so great?"

Now that he's staring right at her, Valerie looks like she might faint. She opens her mouth but no words come out.

"She's Valerie Corelli," I say.

Valerie points at me and nods. She still doesn't seem able to speak.

"I'll pass it on." Max stands and closes the door. "Shall we?"

I take his arm. "You know, she knew you, too. Is it hard being famous?"

He leads us into the dimly lit bar. "My fame is limited to bodybuilding and pickles."

I spot Cam sitting on a stool, surrounded by enough tricked-out muscle to fill a beefcake wall calendar.

"These are all your friends?"

"The boys who work out at Buster's, mainly."

"But not Colt McClure."

He laughs. "No, he's scarce these days. Parker's here, though. Those two are tight."

He points out a short-haired man in a tight, pale-blue polo, his arm wrapped around a petite woman. There's a whole cluster of people clumped next to the bar, half of them sitting on tall stools with their backs against the counter.

"Max!" Another man, who is somehow taller than my cousin, approaches, smacking Max on the shoulder. "Who's this?"

"Nadia. My aunt Caprice's daughter. She just got her MBA, so don't think your dimly lit bulb is going to have a damn thing to say to her."

"Ahh, a brain in the family. I didn't think you Pickles were familiar with that variety." The man nods at me. "I'm Luca. I work out with Max, mainly spotting him when he's too pathetic to make a lift."

Max slides onto a stool next to Camryn. "And Luca's ego grows three sizes every workout, despite the fact that his opponent mopped the floor with him in his last match."

"My first match." Luca settles on a stool next to Max and drags another one forward with his foot for me. "I wasn't as ready as I'd been led to believe."

"You got that right," says Parker, who has turned toward us. "The Lukinator got dropped in forty-six seconds."

I swivel my head between the two men. "Lukinator?"

Max takes a cup from Camryn. "His fighter name. We told him it was going to be bad luck."

"I'm changing it," Luca says. "We should get an outsider's opinion." He grins at me.

"An opinion for what?" I ask.

"The new name."

"I don't think I know anything about fighter names." I nod at Camryn, who is pointing at a frozen margarita machine. I need something if I'm going to manage these completely foreign conversations with outrageously hot men.

"It has to sound fierce," Luca says.

"And not like you lukinated all over the floor," Parker says with a laugh.

"It wasn't a very good choice," says the woman next to him. "And hi, I'm Maddie."

"Nadia."

"You haven't introduced her around," Camryn tells Max, "And I'm having to order her a drink."

Luca stands. "I'll get her a drink."

"Sit down," Max says. "All you punks keep your paws off my cousin."

"Unless she likes their paws," Camryn adds, motioning to the bartender behind her. "Max, we asked her here to meet people, not scare them off."

Max grumbles as Camryn orders a margarita for me and a Sprite for herself.

"Get another margarita for me," Maddie says. "It's the only way I can deal with all these blowhards."

They're all casual in jeans and graphic T-shirts. But everything else about them is beautiful. Carved features. Muscles for days.

I accept my plastic cup of margarita from Camryn and take a sip. Euwww. Dive bar margaritas. Barely drinkable.

Luca shifts on his stool. "Back to my fighter name? I'm thinking of changing it to…" He pauses for emphasis and holds up his hands like he's revealing a marquee. "The Totaler."

"My grandma was a teetotaler," Parker says. "Never drank a drop of booze." Laughter breaks out over the group.

"Or a totaler like an accountant?" Max asks. "Because I can total up the number of times you're going to lose with that name."

Luca frowns. "It's that bad?" He turns to me. "In your unbiased opinion?"

I take another sip to buy me some time. I don't want to insult these people I barely know. "I get what you were going for. You'll total someone. But I think they might be right that there are too many other connotations."

Luca frowns, and I feel bad. "I'm sure we can workshop something." I turn to Parker. "What's your fighter name?"

"Power Play," he says.

"Good one," I say. "Are they usually one word or two?"

"It varies," Max says. "Colt's dad was 'The Cure' and Colt was 'Gunner' because of his fighting style."

I turn to Luca. "What's your style?"

"Loser," Parker says with another laugh.

I almost shoot him a look, but it seems like all these friends are tight, the level of closeness that allows you to insult each other in good fun.

Luca shrugs. "I'm not sure I have a style yet."

"Enough on names," Maddie says. "Who wants to shoot some pool?"

The group wanders over to the back corner of the bar where four pool tables stand, two of them empty. Luca carries my stool. I wonder if he's been assigned to me, or if his attention has warned off the others.

"Shots before shots," Maddie says. She stops a shot server with a holder full of test tubes. "Put them on Max's tab."

"Hey!" Max protests, but hands the woman a card.

A few of the men wave off the shot server. They have fights tomorrow. But most everyone but Cam takes one. So I do, too. So does Luca.

"And down!" Maddie cries.

I chug the shot. I haven't done that in a while. We pile the empty test tubes on the woman's tray.

"I'm going to grab a water," Luca says. "Gotta stay one-to-one on the hydration."

Camryn takes the extra stool. When Luca's gone, she says, "Let me know if he gets too attentive. We can shoo him off you."

"I'm not really in the market for a guy," I say.

"Oh, but these are so pretty."

"Hey!" Max says.

She pats his cheek. "You're the prettiest one."

"He kind of is," I tell her.

Max stands behind Camryn as Maddie racks the balls. It looks as though she and Parker are going to play two of the other fighters.

"That's Hudson, Jo's brother," Camryn says, pointing at a wiry fighter who looks like pure strength.

"Jo?"

"Colt McClure's wife. Hudson's wife Chloe will be here later."

"And the other one?"

"Everyone calls him Hex."

"Is that his fighter name?"

"Yes, and he won't tell anyone his real one." Camryn sips her Sprite and sighs as she rubs her round belly. "I'm wearing out already."

"Can I do anything?" I ask.

"No, it's just random exhaustion that hits unexpectedly. I'll be all right."

Luca returns with his water and a fresh margarita. "For you," he says.

I'm about to protest when I realize I've finished the first one.

"Okay, thanks." I tuck the new cup into the empty.

We watch the pool game. Maddie takes the first shot.

Camryn turns to Luca. "What about 'The Interloper'? Makes you sound like you're pushing your way into the big leagues."

Luca nods. "Not bad."

"What's Hudson's fighter name?" I ask.

"'Reckless,'" Camryn says. "Although I think he started out as 'The Contender.'"

"His sister was 'The Hurricane' before she retired," Luca adds.

"You need to brainstorm synonyms," I say. "Brutal. Fierce. Cut-throat. Ferocious."

"Ferocious," Luca says. "I like that."

"Then add some alliteration," I say.

"A litter of what?" Luca asks.

Max cuffs his shoulder. "I told you she was smart."

"Alliteration," I say again. "Where the first letter is the same. Like Ferocious Fighter. Or Ferocious Fiend."

"Ferocious Fiend." Luca nods. "I like it."

"Keep thinking," I say, not sure I want to be the one to name him in the ring, or the octagon, I guess. "Synonyms plus alliteration."

Luca leans against the painted cinderblock wall, his mind clearly on the names.

Camryn leans in, "I think you've got him distracted."

I shrug and take a sip of my margarita, only to be greeted with air. I finished the second one, too. When did that happen?

Luca hears the sound. "I'll get you another one."

"Oh! I'm not sure I should."

"I'll get it just in case." He takes off.

Camryn winks at me. "He's interested."

"I'm not sure he's my type."

"You're free to meet Hex if you want to," Camryn says, gesturing to the far corner where the other fighter watches Maddie sink the last ball to finish the game.

"No way," Max says. "Hex will try to nail her in the

back alley. He's not going anywhere near my baby cousin."

I punch Max's beefy arm. "I'm not a baby! And maybe I want him to nail me in the back alley!"

"Was I summoned?" Hex lumbers toward us with a smooth, powerful step that looks like it might shake the earth. He's easily the widest of the fighter men, even though I think Max might have an inch of height on him. Even so, I barely reach his chin.

"No," Max says.

"Who's this?" he asks, taking in my bare shoulder, the hint of cleavage over my tank, and my jeans. I feel thoroughly evaluated.

Max steps forward. "My baby cousin Nadia, and if you even look at her the wrong way, I'll break your face."

"With what? Your pretty tan?" Hex laughs. He turns to me. "Happy to nail you in the back alley, but normally I like you to buy me dinner first."

I ought to be intrigued by him, his white T-shirt straining against his chest and the short sleeves doing little to contain crazy biceps that defy the laws of ordinary human physiology.

But I don't think he's my type either. I imagine him over me, and all I can picture is me gasping to breathe under all that muscle.

Luca returns with the new margarita plus another test tube shot, the one I had before. He noticed which one I chose.

This is more attention than I've gotten in a good while.

He passes me the shot. "You seemed to like the last one."

"I did." I salute him with it and down it. I'm hitting my limit. I will sip slowly on the margarita. "Thank you."

"Hey, Hex." Luca says.

"What is it, Pukinator?"

Luca scowls, his face contorting like a toddler. "That's not my name."

"It is for me."

I catch Camryn's eye. She shrugs.

Luca and Hex glare at each other, as if I'm a prize they have to fight over.

I'm not used to this. I take another icky sip and realize I'm stress drinking. That's why I've gone through these so fast, even though they're terrible.

But as I try to think of something to say to either of them, my stomach turns. Great. Cheap tequila and crap ingredients. I grin and bear it, hoping it will settle down.

Hex watches my face with a scrutiny I didn't expect. "You are very beautiful, Nadia, cousin of Max. Do you live in LA?"

Dang, he's direct. "I do." I forget and take another absent-minded sip of the drink and instantly regret it. Bile rises in my throat. Am I going to throw up? Panic courses through me, and I miss whatever Hex says next.

"Excuse me a second." I set the drink on my stool and hurry for the back hall where I spotted a bathroom sign.

Couples are lined up along the walls in the darkened space, hands all over each other.

I push my way through. "Excuse me. Sorry." And as I feel increasingly bad, "Move!"

I barely make it through the door and into a stall before I collapse, throwing up yellow-green margarita into the bowl. What was in those things?

I pick up my phone to text Camryn to come help me. What have I done, drinking them so fast? I know better. And those shots? What type of liquor was it? I chose it for the pretty green color.

My stomach heaves, and I throw up again. Ugh. This is the worst.

My eyes water and burn as mascara melts into them. My phone beeps with a text and in my rush to lift my head to look at it, I smack it on the metal box attached to the wall.

Shit, shit, shit!

I feel weak, throwing up again into the blurry bowl. I can't hold myself up. I sink to the floor.

I have to tell Camryn. Or Max.

I fumble with my phone, blinking to clear my vision. But it's no good, so I give up on texting and put through a call to my most recent contact. It should be Cam from when she told me what to wear.

The line connects, and a voice comes on. "Nadia?"

It's not Camryn. It's Dalton.

"Sorry, I meant to call…"

And I puke again. I gasp into the bowl. Jesus. What is going on? I feel awful, like I'm dying.

"Nadia? Are you at the bar?"

"I'm sick," I choke out. "It's bad."

Then I clutch my stomach and drop the phone to the floor.

I can't stop throwing up.

DALTON

I stare at the phone.

"Nadia?"

She doesn't answer.

The call is still going. I can hear muffled music and talking. It's echoing, like she's in a small room.

"Nadia? What's going on? Where are you?"

Then the call ends.

Fuck.

She sounded in great distress.

Where did she say she was going?

Did she tell me?

I pace our apartment as I scroll through the text messages.

She said she'd be out tonight and not to worry if I wasn't home when I got in from my shift.

I keep scrolling. Then I find it.

Aces. A bar in East LA.

I grab my keys and race to lock up and jump into my Jeep.

Where is her cousin? What's happened?

I slam my hand against the steering wheel as I drive across town, ignoring all speed limits and turning any yellow light into a reason to gun it.

She might not even be at the bar anymore. It's almost midnight. Someone could have taken her somewhere. She could be in real danger.

"Shit!"

There's no way I can track her. We don't have that level of connection. I have to hope she's at Aces.

I think about the call. The music would get louder, then fade again. It's a bathroom at the bar. I'm almost sure of it.

She went in there, then … what? She said she was sick.

The light turns red, but I don't care. I gun through it, swerving to miss the car that starts through the intersection.

It honks at me. I don't care about that either.

We get a slew of over-intoxicated people at the ER every weekend. She'll be okay. She might need her stomach pumped. IV fluids.

Unless she's allergic to something.

Or somebody at the bar drugged her.

Fuck. FUCK!

I finally reach the block of the bar. There's no parking anywhere.

Fuck it. I pull onto the sidewalk and slam the door. Tow the car. I don't care.

Thankfully, there's no line to get in, and no bouncer outside to notice my shitty parking.

I yank on the door.

The noise hits me. It's crowded.

I scan the faces, looking for her. She's not going to be out here.

And I don't know her cousin. We've never met. I couldn't spot him either.

The bathroom. I have to find that.

I sure as hell hope she's in there.

The back corner has a hallway, and I head for it. There's a crowd here, too, and a line to get in.

"Hey!" some woman says, pulling at me as I skip them and tug on the door.

I jerk away from her and head inside.

Several women at the mirrors turn to gape at me.

"Nadia?" I call out. "Are you in here?"

The noise matches what I heard earlier. This is it. I know it.

There are three stalls, all closed.

I drop to my knees.

I see her instantly, curled over the toilet, her legs crumpled beneath her.

"Shit, Nadia!"

The door is locked, but I kick it, holding the top so it won't slam into her.

The wood splinters, and it opens.

"Jesus, man!" The women scatter.

I pull her off the toilet. "Nadia?" I lightly smack her cheek to bring her around. "Nadia?"

She finally stirs. "Dalton?"

Shit. She's weak as a kitten.

The floor is filthy, so I pull off my shirt and lay it on

the ground. Then I carefully pry her off the toilet to rest on top of my shirt.

Her hair fans out. She's pale. Her eyes flutter. "So sick."

I feel her pulse. Slow. Her skin is clammy.

I use my phone as light and check her pupils. They react normally. So she's probably not drugged. Just too much booze.

I sigh in relief. "How much did you have?"

Tears leak out of her eyes. Her mascara is smeared.

A hefty man bursts into the bathroom to loom over us. "What the fuck, man?"

"Call an ambulance," I tell him. "Right now. She's weak from throwing up. She'll need an IV, maybe her stomach pumped. Her pulse is low."

"Are you a doctor or what?"

I gesture to my pants scrubs. "Yes." Every long shift is worth it, because I've seen a lot of people like Nadia. I know what to do.

The man looks us over, Nadia on the floor. "Shit." He punches on his phone.

A woman with a riot of black braids peers in. "Can I help?"

"Could you wet some paper towels?"

She hurries toward the sinks.

"She's not dead, right?" the man asks.

Jesus. "No, she's not dead."

"Sorry, is she yours?"

"She's my roommate."

The man talks into the phone, then nods at me. "Ambulance is coming."

I check Nadia's pulse again. Still weak and slow. It seems like the vomiting is done.

I hadn't pegged her for a party girl.

Another woman bursts into the bathroom. She's pregnant. "Nadia?" she calls. "Are you in here? You've been gone—" She spots us, and her hand covers her mouth. "Nadia!"

She kneels next to us. "What happened?"

"She called me. She was throwing up."

"Is she okay? She doesn't look okay!"

"She's all right. We've called an ambulance."

"Oh my god!" She clutches her belly. "Oooh!"

Now I have two women in distress on my hands. "Deep breaths. Slow down and breathe."

She nods, taking in long, jagged breaths.

"Are you the pregnant woman she lived with? Allergic to cats?"

"Yes! Who are you?" She takes in my naked chest.

"Dalton. Her roommate."

"Her … what?"

Uh oh. I didn't realize Nadia had kept me a secret. "We're friends. Sharing a space. She called me. She'll be okay."

The woman takes in more jagged breaths.

Then a man races in, pushing people aside. He's huge. "Camryn? Did you find her?"

This is bound to be the cousin.

I turn to explain things, but then I'm lifted by my waistband. "What the fuck did you do to Nadia?"

Camryn pummels his leg. "Max! Put him down! It's

Nadia's roommate! And look at him! He's wearing scrubs. Are you a doctor?"

Any second, the flimsy string holding up my pants together is going to break. Damn, this guy is strong. "I'm Dr. Dalton Murphy. Let me the fuck down."

Max lowers me again. "Shit. Sorry."

The first woman passes me wet paper towels over the pregnant woman's head. "Here. Sorry. This is crazy."

I take them. "Thank you."

I wipe the wad of towels over Nadia's brow, across her neck, and press it into her wrists.

Camryn's voice is full of fear. "She's sick, Max. She called her roommate."

"Wait, her roommate?" His eyes rove over me.

I focus back on Nadia.

"They're friends," Camryn says.

"She has a friend here?"

I can't explain and don't know how much I should explain. This is Nadia's situation. Her eyes are closed.

"Nadia?" I shake her shoulders. "Are you with us?"

She moans. "Yes."

The temperature rises as more people crowd into the room. I look up to see additional men as tricked out as this one, and some of them even more. Good grief. Did someone call a SWAT team?

"Who are all these people?" I ask.

"Our friends," Camryn says. "They're fighters."

"Did you call an ambulance?" Max booms.

"First thing," I say. "We might have to pump her stomach, get her some fluids. I'll keep close watch."

"Oh, God. I should have slowed her down." Camryn starts crying.

Max wraps an arm around her. "She's a grown woman capable of choosing her drinks."

Nadia lurches up. "I'm going to throw up again."

"On your side so you won't aspirate," I tell her. "You're too weak to get up." I pull her hair out of the way.

She coughs and heaves, but nothing comes out. She's gotten it out.

"Jesus Christ." Max turns around. "Where is the fucking ambulance?"

But I hear the terse instructions. "Move aside, please. Let us through."

That's the paramedics.

"Back up. Let them get her loaded," I say. I slide Nadia to her back again.

Max, Camryn, and I move aside as the two men enter the bathroom.

"Dr. Murphy?" one says. I recognize him from the ER. He came in a couple of hours ago with a heart attack patient.

"I'm her roommate," I say. "She called me."

"What happened?"

The other one kneels beside Nadia to take her vitals.

"Looks like regular alcohol poisoning. No definitive sign of toxins, but I'm sure they'll run a panel to be sure. She called me. It took me a good ten minutes to get here."

The other man stands. "Let's get her loaded." He turns to me. "You coming with us?"

I glance over at Max.

Camryn takes his arm. "Let him go, Max. He's a doctor. We can follow."

Max nods.

They load Nadia onto the stretcher and strap her in. When they lift her, her eyes flutter open. "Dalton?"

She asked for me.

I throw my shirt back on. I've had worse on it in the ER. "I'm here. You're all right, Nadia. We've got you."

"Dalton?" Nadia asks again. Now she's confused. "Where's Max and Cam?"

Okay, so she maybe didn't mean to call me.

"We're here," Camryn says with a cry. "Nadia!"

"I'm okay," she says. "I think it was bad tequila."

"We're taking you to the hospital," the paramedic says.

"Okay." Nadia closes her eyes. "I might throw up again."

"We'll take care of you," I tell her. "Don't worry."

She reaches out for me, and I take her hand.

Maybe she did call me? It doesn't matter. I'm here.

The two paramedics push forward toward the door.

"We'll go to South General," I tell Max and Camryn. "Come find us."

"We will," Camryn says.

"Keep her hydrated," I tell Max. "She might have contractions if she's distressed."

He nods.

And with that, I follow the paramedics through the crowd of Aces, my hand clasped around Nadia's.

13

NADIA

I don't end up getting my stomach pumped.

I throw up three times on the ride over, not that much of anything comes out, and by the time they check my blood levels, I'm already recovering.

They won't let Max and Cam stay in my curtained space for more than a hug, but Dalton gets to remain. The IV fluids have an anti-nausea drug in them, and I start feeling better.

"Do you remember how much you drank?" Dalton asks.

This is embarrassing.

"I was in the middle of my third margarita. And I had two shots."

"How fast?"

"Pretty fast." I can't look in his direction, instead focusing on the wavy pattern on the curtain.

"You didn't strike me as the binge drinking type."

"I'm not."

"Hey."

I turn to him.

"I'm not judging you. Just asking the questions that need to be asked if we're going to be sure you're okay."

"I'm fine." I look away again.

"You seem better."

This is the worst. I'm not like this. I was out of my element, and people kept handing me drinks.

Ugh.

The doctor who saw me first comes in. He knows Dalton. I can tell by the smirk on his face, but they don't let on in front of me. "Your blood panel came back clear on Rohypnol, GHP, and Ketamine, which are the usual date-rape drugs. But your blood alcohol level was .2, which is high."

"I thought dive bars would be skimpy on the alcohol," I say.

"Not that one." He leans forward and uses a penlight to look into my eyes again. "You still feeling nauseous?"

"No. Just tired."

He lifts the IV bag, which is almost empty. "Good. We'll get you out of here. Your discharge instructions are plenty of fluids and rest, and maybe no dive bars for a while." His gaze flicks over to Dalton and his eyebrows lift.

"Got it."

When he leaves, I turn to Dalton. "You know him, don't you?"

"Not well. He's an attending, but not my direct supervisor."

The thought that I could get Dalton in trouble for

being here with me sends a spike of anxiety through me. "Is it okay that you're here? Max can take me home."

Dalton doesn't get a chance to answer, because a new nurse in pink scrubs comes in, cute and perky despite the hour. "I have discharge papers. Oh!" She spots Dalton. "You're here!"

I look between them. They seem more familiar than him and the doctor.

"This is my roommate," he says.

"Roommate, huh?" She passes a clipboard to me.

I don't want to say anything. It's bad enough that Dalton thinks I'm a lush, but now other people who know him will think it, too.

I scribble my name on the pages and thrust the clipboard back at her.

"I didn't know you lived with someone," the nurse says to Dalton. It's like I'm not there. Something is happening here.

I watch Dalton to see how he's managing this conversation, if this situation is affecting a burgeoning romance.

"We got a place about a month ago."

She presses the clipboard to her chest. "Known each other long?"

"A while," he says. "Is someone going to remove the IV? I don't think I have clearance to do it off hours."

She huffs. "I'll send someone in." She spins on her heels, her blond ponytail swinging.

Now it's Dalton who stares at the curtains.

"Love interest?" I ask.

"No."

"I think she's interested. Or was." I pick at my white tank. It's tight and revealing all by itself. The red cardigan will have to be hosed down. I might toss it after this.

"Maybe." He rubs his neck. He's bound to be exhausted, coming off a long shift only to end up back here.

"I'm sorry if I screwed things up for you."

That gets his attention. "With Sonya? No. Don't worry about that. Or do you mean sleeping?"

"I mean all the things. I meant to call Camryn. I couldn't stop puking long enough to look at my phone."

"I'm glad you called."

"Were you off shift?"

"I was home."

The word seems to hang in the curtained space. I have a home with him. I've had roommates before, but this feels different. We collaborate on how we set it up. We make meals together.

We're grownups, not college students.

Although maybe I acted like one tonight.

"Do you want me to talk to Sonya?" I say it with some trepidation. I don't want to, but then I can't have my awful night make things worse for him. "I can assure her I'm not anyone important to you."

His face looks pained. "No, no. She's just a nurse I know." He waves it away.

My phone beeps. It's a text from Max.

I read it quickly. "He needs to take Camryn home.

He wants to know if my roommate, all caps, will get me to the apartment." I let out a long gust of air. Of course they know now. "You told them?"

Dalton sighs. "Yeah, I'm afraid I let that cat out of the bag. I didn't know you hadn't said anything."

"Probably a fair trade for my secret cat *in* the bag. I'll have to deal with it later." I text Max that I'm good and to go home, and set the phone down.

"My car's illegally parked at Aces, but we can call for a ride home," Dalton says.

"What did you do with your poor Jeep?"

"I may or may not have driven onto the sidewalk."

"You're going to get towed!"

"Possibly."

I sit back against the pillow. He was worried. He cares about me. Still, something about Sonya niggles at me. She seemed to expect that he was single, and something about what she saw suggested that he wasn't.

"I'm guessing no one knows you have a roommate, either? A female one?"

He rubs his neck again. "It hasn't come up."

A man in scrubs strolls in like it's a house party, his shoulders rolling like he's vibing to music only he can hear. "Dr. D, didn't expect to see you here."

Dalton smiles. "Nadia, this is Joaquin. Best IV guy in the ER. This is my roommate Nadia."

"I've heard." He expertly pulls the IV, adhesive and all, so quickly and painlessly that I don't realize it's gone until he's taped a cotton ball on my arm. "Everyone thinks you have a secret piece, and that's why you haven't taken out anyone on the floor."

My head whips to Dalton. "Secret piece?"

"I can't help what they say," Dalton says. "Let's get you sitting up." He presses into my back until I'm forward off the pillow. "How does that feel? No return of the nausea?"

I shake my head.

"Swing your legs around slowly. Let's make sure you're steady."

"Looks like you've got this, Dr. D. When's your next shift?"

"About twenty hours."

"Get some shut-eye. I'll see you on the flip side." Joaquin rolls the IV out of the space.

My head is whirling with everything that's happened, from the fighters, to the sickness, the ride with Dalton in the ambulance, and now, realizing he's a hot commodity at work and he's not taking anyone up on it.

"Socks on the floor," he says. "Let's give standing a go, then we'll get your shoes back on."

"I'm fine," I say, but when I shift my weight off the bed, my legs feel like Jell-O. I clutch Dalton's arms. "Or maybe not."

"You need some food. Wait here. I'll wheel you out." He sets me back on the bed.

While he's gone, I move the plastic bag with my dirty cardigan to my lap and set my tiny crossbody bag on top of it.

I'm going to need some food, some sleep, and a much clearer head to sort through all the fallout from this disaster of a night. My cousin knows about my roommate. My roommate had to save me.

And for some reason, everyone except the two of us seems to think there is something going on.

But as Dalton returns with a wheelchair and carefully lowers me into it, I start to think—maybe I called the right person after all.

14

DALTON

I do not get a full eight hours of sleep before I have to return to the hospital for work.

But Nadia is home and comfortable. I was able to keep checking on her and make sure we didn't miss anything in the ER.

And I slept some, a handful of hours.

Catzilla curls up behind Nadia's knees as I ease the door open to leave for an overnight shift. "Watch over her," I whisper to the kitty.

The cat lifts her head to acknowledge me, then sets it down again.

I stand in the open doorway, taking a moment to look over the space. The kitchen is softly lit by the bulb over the sink, sending a glow that almost, but not quite, reaches the bed.

Nadia's hair is spilled over her arms, only her face visible above the ruffled edge of her blue comforter. Catzilla's ears twitch as if she's annoyed I'm still there.

It's a peaceful scene compared to the chaos of the

bar, then the hospital. We took an Uber to my car, which thankfully hadn't been towed or even ticketed yet, and came home.

If we were going to have a first disaster together, at least this one resolved easily enough.

I quietly close the door.

When I arrive at South General, Farraday, who was the attending with Nadia last night, is on his way home.

"You have your hands full with that one," he says, slamming his locker closed.

"She's just a roommate."

"That you literally gave your shirt for." He shrugs out of his white coat.

"I thought she'd been drugged."

Farraday shoulders his bag. "She's lucky she wasn't. Or else there's something else out there that doesn't show on a panel."

"She's not a big drinker. She had a lot. I think she was pressured by some new companions."

"Shitty companions."

"Probably." I do have a bone to pick with her cousin, but I'm not going to tell Farraday that.

"See you around." He heads out of the room.

Harrington peeks around the row of metal lockers, only his buzzed black hair and glasses visible. "What's going on?"

Right. My intern group has been off, so they haven't caught up on the latest news.

I reach for my badge and tug it off the hook. "Nothing important."

Fitz, short for Fitzsimmons, a perennially sunny

intern from SoCal, drops onto the bench. She pulls off her cap to an explosion of blond curls. "I heard Sonya is fit to be tied that Dalton here has a live-in when she planned to sink her talons into him."

That was fast. "How did you hear that?"

Fitz unzips her bag. "I went to the cafeteria for coffee. Jessica R heard it from Jessica G who got it from Sonya herself before she went off shift."

"So glad to be the source of hospital gossip," I say, closing my locker with less of a slam than Farraday did.

Fitz playfully sweeps out her foot in pink crocs to trip me as I go by. "It's hard being the most eligible intern at South General." She stuffs her bag in her locker.

"Hey!" Harrington says, clipping his badge to the pocket of his scrubs. "I'm single!"

Fitz forces a smile at him, then puts an arm around each of us as we head out to the unit. "Harrington, we need to get you a makeover."

He pushes his glasses higher on his nose. "Really?"

"Really. We need to make you less Urkle and more Idris Elba."

"You think it's possible?"

Fitz laughs. "Anything is possible."

When we enter the back hall of the ER, it's chaos. Typical Saturday night.

Booker, our supervisor, starts fanning us out. "Harrington, take the broken arm in Bay 3. Fitz, we have a respiratory in Bay 5." She smirks at me before she says, "Murphy, I hear you're good with the binge drinkers. You have a puker in Bay 9. Go!"

We scatter, but not before I realize maybe I should

have had the ambulance take Nadia to any hospital other than South General.

When I open the curtain to Bay 9, Dr. Clemons is in there with a nurse I don't know. "Good, you take over. Order the standard panel for high blood alcohol. You do know what that is?"

"Yes, sir."

The nurse glances up, holding a long, narrow vomit basin next to the man. "Your turn. I have six patients I'm behind on."

I take the basin.

The man leans over and vomits violently. I shift the basin to catch most of it, but some hits the floor.

"And clean that up!" the nurse says as she closes the curtain.

It's good to be an intern.

Things finally calm down in the wee hours. It's been a night, even for LA. Four car accidents, and at least twenty people presenting with some stomach flu. Plus, my alcohol case. Six others came in, and every single one was given to me.

I sit with Harrington and Fitz in the break room, none of us really eating what is technically lunch, even though it's four a.m.

"So much puke tonight," Fitz says. "Do you think we'll ever get used to the puke?"

"I'm ready to have more clout than an orderly," I say.

Fitz rests her head on her hands. "With great power comes great responsibility."

"I'll be nice."

"Unlike eighty percent of the attendings." Fitz closes her eyes.

"We do seem to have a lot of egos on our floor." Harrington takes off his glasses and wipes them on his scrubs.

"So tell us about your woman," Fitz says with a yawn. "Other than she's a party animal who hangs out at dive bars."

I had a feeling this was coming.

"It's a roommate thing. She needed a place. I needed a place. We're sharing an apartment."

"That's boring," Fitz says. "Surely you've got something you can confess about her."

That I like being around her? That I think she's ungodly beautiful, even laid out on a bathroom floor? That I know she's smarter than I am, despite her working at a deli with an MBA and me in a med program?

I'm not saying any of that.

"She can cook. She lets me eat the leftovers."

"Marry that girl," Harrington says. "Marry her now."

Fitz flicks a balled up straw wrapper at him. "Women are more than personal cooks."

"I know!" Harrington says. "Most of them don't cook at all anymore. Marry this one! Act fast!"

I manage a short laugh. "I think I need to be more financially solvent to marry anyone."

"Right. You pay for mom back home." Fitz closes her eyes. "Wake me when our phones go off." She lays her head of unruly curls on her arms.

Harrington looks at her longingly. I don't say anything about it. I get the whole unrequited business.

Not that I have unrequited feelings for Nadia.

I don't.

Fitz gets approximately ninety seconds of rest when her phone dings. Then Harrington, then me.

"There's lunch," Harrington says, belatedly cramming half a sandwich in his mouth.

I force a couple of bites of noodles down and return my lunch bag to the fridge.

Then we're off again, ready to handle another round of emergencies.

And hopefully done with the gossip about my roommate.

15

NADIA

I mostly put off Max and Camryn when I get home. I return their worried texts and promise that Dalton is keeping watch over me.

Camryn in particular feels distraught because she feels the group pressured me into drinking. Max wants to wring Luca's neck for continuously bringing me margaritas and a second shot.

But they don't know where I live, so it's not hard to dodge them until Sunday when I arrive at the deli for a shift.

When I walk in, they're both there waiting as the rest of the staff preps the restaurant to open for lunch.

Camryn rushes forward to throw her arms around me. "When I realized how long you had been gone, I was beside myself. I should have gone with you."

"It's fine. I was in a big hurry to avoid puking in front of all your friends."

Max growls low in his throat. "I've already had

words with Luca about how much liquor he forced on you."

I pull back from Camryn to stare him in the eye. "He didn't make me drink them. And he didn't make me take the first *or* second shot."

Camryn holds my wrist. She doesn't seem to want to let go of me, as if it might happen all over again. "Our group runs fast and loose. I should have been more attentive."

"You were exhausted, if you recall."

"Well, no more dive bars for us," Max says. "The last thing I wanted when we invited you was for you to get peer pressured into binge drinking."

"I'm fine. I'm a grown adult."

The other employees skirt us, but I can tell they are taking far too much interest in our conversation. Jeannie arrives with a bin of chopped pickles, and I take that as my opportunity to get to work.

"What needs chopping?" I ask her, watching as she sets the bin into the refrigerated sandwich line.

"We need carrots and cabbage for the pickled slaw," she says.

I follow her to the kitchen as she continues listing items. "And I'm going to need more pickle quarter slices in regular, spicy, and garlic."

"I'm on it." I shove my purse into my locker and pull out my apron. A quick glance through the window in the door between the restaurant and the back shows me that Max and Cam haven't left their spot by the entrance.

Hopefully, that conversation is over.

I head into the walk-in fridge to grab a stack of carrots, then wash them and don a pair of gloves.

As I arrange the vegetables on the chopping table to be prepped, I wonder if I should have asked Max not to tell his dad or mine about the bar incident.

Probably he won't. To him, he looks as at fault as I am.

And besides, we're not kids. Nobody needs to be running to Daddy.

I take out my frustration on the carrots, chopping the tops and running a peeler down the sides. I'm not even a college student anymore more. I pay my own bills, meager though they are. If I want to spend my MBA on slicing carrots, it's my MBA to use as I like.

Who says I need to always overachieve? Maybe I enjoy prepping vegetables!

I do, actually, getting into a rhythm that quickly fills a bowl for the slaw. I slide the scraps into the compost at the end of the wood block and return to the fridge for the cabbage.

I know I'm not meant for a job like this. It's not what I went to school for. But it's honest work, and necessary. And Max can rely on me when he needs to be out.

Although maybe my reliability score dropped substantially after Friday night.

I slice through the cabbage. I'm not a fan of the pickle slaw, but I don't mind making it. It goes on the pickled roast beef, a monthly special dubbed "The Beefy Pickle."

Now that's a name for one of my romance novels.

And somehow, that line of thought takes me right back to Dalton.

Jeannie takes a spot opposite me at the table, setting a bin of garlic pickles onto the surface with a thunk. "I'm going to start quartering."

She's the kitchen manager, only a couple of years older than me. She is doing what she's meant to do, having graduated culinary school. Like my cousin Anthony, she likes to create new dishes for the deli.

But despite her age and the adorable smattering of freckles that make her seem approachable, she's an unyielding stickler when it comes to food prep. Get the size or texture wrong, and she'll make you start all over, no matter how many people might be lined up waiting for slaw or potato salad or the pickle of the month.

"Watch that cabbage," she says. "Between one-eighth and one-sixteenth of an inch. You're getting wide."

"Gotcha."

Point made.

A voice rings out from the restaurant. "Doors!" It's Margo, the weekend manager. She's letting us know the deli is officially open.

Jeannie and I chop in companionable silence as Vera and Frank move the last items from the fridge to the line. Jeannie's already sliced all the bread they baked this morning.

It's quiet for a while, and a quick glance shows that the first customers have arrived. I don't do much out there if I can help it. I prefer the sanctuary of the chopping block.

The kitchen door swings open, and Max comes in, followed by, of all people, Hex.

"Strange man in my kitchen!" Jeannie protests, holding her oversized butcher knife at both the men. It's almost comical, the freckled woman in her low white hat, and the two giants she's threatening.

"I'm sorry, Jeannie," Max says. "I know you don't like non-employees in here."

"Wash up or I'll cut off your hands!" She waves the knife at them, and both Max and Hex scurry to the sinks along the wall.

I bite back a smile. Jeannie is a force of nature.

When the two men are clean and dry, Jeannie looks up from her pickles. "What brings you two in here?"

"It's for Nadia," Max says.

I look up. Me?

"Whatever for?" I ask.

"I feel like I should have noticed you were in distress," Hex says, holding his outrageously bear-like hand over his chest. It rests on the words, "Pound or get pounded" on his T-shirt.

"How would you have known?" I ask. Dang, this guy is huge. He's wider than the chopping table. Jeannie pays him no mind now.

"We were talking when you left in such a hurry," Hex says.

Right. I had been. I forgot that he and Luca were having a Nadia pissing match.

"It's fine." I wave my knife as if to push away the thought. "I think I'll revert to my weekends at home for a while."

Max nudges his arm.

Hex clears his throat. "I was wondering if you'd give me the honor of a date. No drinking necessary. Unless you want to. I mean, in moderation."

Jeannie stops chopping to look at me.

Oh, gosh.

"Hex, I mean, wow, you're great, but I want to lie low for a while. If that's okay. I think I should, you know, take a breather from going out."

Jeannie bites her lip like she's trying not to laugh at the big lug trying to be contrite.

"Not a problem," Hex says. "I shot my shot." He turns to Jeannie and says, "I apologize for disturbing your very clean and organized kitchen."

Dang, the jolly giant can be a gentleman.

Jeannie frowns at him. "Fine. Now the two of you get out of here!" She picks up her knife again.

But Hex is watching her with amusement. "Do you always threaten bodily harm on people?"

"Only when their un-aproned, unapproved, sweaty bodies are near my prep space!"

"I also cause bodily harm to people."

That stops Jeannie in her tracks. "Really?" She turns to Max. "And you let him ask out your cousin?"

"It's not like that," Max says.

"Out!" Jeannie says, moving her knife closer. "Out of my kitchen, you brutes!" She shakes her head.

"We should go," Max says. He pushes Hex out the door.

As soon as they're gone, I start laughing.

"What?" Jeannie asks.

"You scared off over four hundred pounds of solid muscle."

"And I'd do it again." She glances at my cabbage. "Stop chopping! Nobody's going to eat that much slaw in a day."

I shake my head, but I move the cut cabbage to a bin and pick up the extra heads to return to the fridge.

This has been the wildest afternoon.

But the funny thing is, the main thing I want to do is tell Dalton all about it.

16

DALTON

Nadia and I have crossover time again on the Wednesday night after her eventful weekend at the ER. She cooks a tray of stuffed manicotti and even bakes a pie. Apple, which happened to be the answer to a question she asked me earlier in the week. She wanted to know which flavor was my favorite.

"What's the occasion?" I ask, sitting at the bar as she serves up the manicotti with a thick slice of garlic toast.

"You coming to get me out of a bar bathroom?" She fills two glasses with water. "You didn't have to."

"I was glad I could. It would have been much harder if I was still on shift. And I had no way of contacting your cousins."

She sits next to me. "It's not something that will happen again. I've sworn off drinking for the next decade."

I sink my fork into the glorious pasta resting on a bed of marinara. "This looks incredible."

"I got the recipe from Jeannie at work. She's a real chef who went to culinary school."

The bite fills my mouth with tomato, cheese, and basil. It's glorious. When I swallow, I say, "So good."

"Jeannie can do anything. Funny that she stays at Max's deli even though she could go anywhere. Her father is a big deal in the LA culinary scene."

"Maybe she's like you. Figuring things out." I take another bite. Damn. I could eat this all night.

"Max's deli seems to be filled with workers with secondary ambitions. He's a bodybuilder, of course. But Frank is in a barbershop quartet. He's talented. And Vera did modeling when she was younger, until they expected her to get tall and she didn't."

"You're making friends there."

"Sure. It's a fun group. It's Max. He's a great boss, and he attracts good people."

We eat in companionable silence for a while. Nadia spots me eyeing the pie and slides it forward to cut a slice. She's about to move a piece to a plate when her phone buzzes.

She glances over at it. "Oh, boy."

"Something bad?"

"My Uncle Sherman." She says it with a sigh.

"The one trying to get you to work for him?"

"The one and only."

She hits a button to accept the call but leaves it on speaker so she can tend to the pie. "Hello, Uncle Sherman."

"Nadia! My beautiful niece! How are things in sunny California?"

She lifts the pie slice onto a clean plate and pushes it toward me with a rueful look. "It's great! I've been helping Max. I guess you heard they are having a girl?"

"I did. How delightful. A new pickle on the way. How is his deli?"

"Busy. I cover shifts when he goes to doctor visits."

I press the edge of my fork through the crust of the pie. She's pushing the helping-her-cousin angle.

"That's great. He has a good crew. I'm sure your help is appreciated."

"I think so." She cuts an even bigger piece of pie for herself. Either she's not paying attention or she's a stress eater. I can feel her tension rising. It's in how tightly she holds the knife. The way she keeps shifting on the stool.

"Well, I've been talking to your brother Rhett down at Dougherty. He says the Florida division is growing quickly, and they could sure use another leadership position in marketing. Or operations, if that's your preference."

I pause in my eating. There's that pressure Nadia was hoping to dodge. I wonder if I should give her privacy for this conversation.

Her gaze meets mine. I point to the door.

She shakes her head. "I'm not sure I know what the difference would be." She sets down the knife. The slice is still in the pie plate.

"Oh, I'm sure Rhett could give you the rundown. Why don't I get you a flight to Miami, say, next week?"

That cranked up the heat. I take another bite and watch Nadia's expression. She's in deli mode, ponytail, no makeup, jeans, and a T-shirt. It might be my favorite Nadia look.

"Uncle Sherman," she finally says. "I'm committed to helping Max and Camryn while she's pregnant, and probably for a month or two after."

"Grammy Alma will undoubtedly come to help once the baby is born." The man's voice is gruff. He's used to getting his way.

She draws in a deep breath and I wonder what bomb she's about to drop. She looks like she's prepping one.

Then it comes. "I already signed a lease for an apartment here."

The other line is silent.

Our gazes meet again. I make an exaggerated grimace.

She shrugs, then stares at the phone.

"I see," he says. "So you will be there, what, six months?"

Nadia drops the next bomb. "A year."

"A year in Max's deli? With your education?"

"It was good enough for Grammy. And you, if you recall."

Ooooh. She's really hammering it home.

"Your Grammy and I worked hard so that you could have better lives!"

"I enjoy working in the family deli, Uncle Sherman. And…" She falters, as if she might not want to say what she's about to.

I give her a big thumbs up for encouragement.

"And look what happened with Court. He was miserable."

I wonder what happened to Court. And who is Court?

Silence again.

Our gazes meet. I like this. It feels like a battle we're fighting together. I lean over the counter to move her giant slice of pie onto a plate. She's going to need this in a minute.

"I see," Sherman says. "Well, take your time in LA. We will revisit this conversation after the baby is born."

"Okay. Talk to you then." She pushes end call with a hard jab.

When the line is clearly disconnected, we both start talking at once.

"Whoa! That Uncle Sherman!"

"My uncle is something!"

We both laugh.

I push her pie toward her. "You earned this."

"I did." She picks up her fork and stabs a loose slice of apple. "Looks like I have a reprieve."

"You negotiated like a boss. You didn't back down for a minute."

She grins at me. "I did. Whew! I've been dreading that conversation."

"Who is Court?"

"My brother. He has not enjoyed the Pickle world."

"I see. And you're worried it will happen to you?"

"Not likely, but I'm taking my time making my decisions. Thanks for being a silent cheerleader." She reaches out and squeezes my wrist.

Her cool hand on me is like a jolt of electricity. I give myself a second to absorb it before saying, "Any time."

We resume our pie.

When I think this evening can't get more surprising, she says, "Did you feel that weird jolt when I grabbed your arm?"

Oh. She felt it, too.

I set down my fork. "Yeah."

"It wasn't static electricity."

I shake my head. Where is this going? "No, that is different."

"What is that, like, physiologically? Do you know?"

Okay, that's an unexpected direction. "It's a powerful combination of two neurotransmitters, dopamine and oxytocin. Both are very fast acting. Lots of people describe it as a shock or jolt."

"Is it normal for both people to feel it?"

"That's more the realm of psychology than what I study," I say. "But I know that one person's amygdala can definitely affect another's."

"Amygdala?"

"It's a tiny part of your brain that controls emotions. So if one person's amygdala goes haywire, like if they get explosively mad, say, after someone breaks something, then it's far more likely the other people around them will also get their amygdalas activated."

"What if that person stays calm?"

"Then yes, their calm amygdala will influence the others. You see it a lot in children. If you get upset when they fall, they cry. But if you play it off, so do they. They can mimic the calmness in their parents because their fight or flight didn't get activated."

"And it works for this electricity thing?"

"That's a bit more complicated. If I was not attracted, let's say I'm married and happy, and a cute girl touches my arm, it's less likely that I will feel the same spark she does."

"Or if you're just plain not attracted."

"Sure."

"Do you think both of us feeling it means we are both attracted?"

Nadia is very focused as she asks, like we're talking about trigonometry. "Probably. We're both single. We're getting to know each other. You're ungodly beautiful."

"What?"

"You have to know that."

"I don't think I do. But you think so?"

I'm pretty sure she's not fishing for compliments. She's taking this entire line of logic very seriously. "Everybody thinks so."

"I seriously doubt that. But okay, so you think I'm ungodly beautiful, or whatever, and I think you're stupidly sexy, especially after that shower moment, and so when I touched you, those two neurotransmitters went nuts and created what feels like a spark?"

Wait a minute.

"You think I'm stupidly sexy?"

"Everyone does."

"I'm not sure about that."

"I am. That's beside the point. Do you think it's okay that we live together?"

Uh oh. This is a left turn. "I mean, sure. We've done fine so far."

She taps her fork against her plate, staring off. "You're right. It will be okay."

"It's chemistry. We have a prefrontal cortex for a reason. We don't have to jump each other just because our amygdalas generated dopamine and oxytocin."

She nods. "You're right. We don't have to act on a random spark."

But when she turns back to me, her eyes go straight to my mouth. And mine go to hers.

We stay like that, only a couple of feet apart on the stools.

Should I lean in?

Is she leaning in?

I can barely breathe. Should we do this? Kiss? What will that lead to?

And will it end with one of us out on our ass since we live together?

She seems to be holding her breath.

Then an alarm goes off.

We both jump out of our skins.

My phone is buzzing so hard that it moves on the surface of the bar. I smash my hand on it, trying to push the button to shut it off, but it scoots out of my way.

Finally, I pick it up and turn it off.

Nadia turns back to her plate. "Time for your shift?"

"Yeah."

She stabs a bite of pie. "Take some leftovers for your break."

It's as if none of this ever happened. The conversation, the touch, the spark, the almost-kiss.

I want to address it. Talk about the elephant in the room.

But Nadia drags one of her romance novels toward her. She doesn't hide the title. *Random Acts of Crazy* by Julia Kent.

But we're doing the opposite of that. Random acts of self-control.

I guess it's for the best.

I stand up and head to the cabinets for a container.

Did we miss out on something spectacular?

Or did we get saved from a huge mistake?

17

NADIA

On Saturday morning, Dalton stumbles into the apartment after his shift, dead on his feet.

I'm eating yogurt at the bar, and my eyebrows lift as I watch him drag himself to the dresser for clothes. He usually showers first thing when he gets in. "Rougher night than usual?"

"Yeah. Ten-car pileup. We got about half of the casualties."

My stomach turns. "That's terrible."

"It was grim." His expression tells me that not everybody made it.

"I'm so sorry, Dalton. Is that the hardest part of the job?"

"Telling family that we failed to save someone they love? Might be. I don't do that part yet, but I am expected to be in the room."

I set down my spoon. "That's hard."

He leans against the wall by the bathroom door. "In the moment of trying to help them, you don't think about it. You're following a protocol. But when that adrenaline drops…" He runs his hand over his eyes.

"Get a shower. Then some sleep. I'm going to walk the neighborhood since it's not as hot today."

He nods. "Good. Sunshine helps." He gives a lopsided half-smile, even if the pain is still in his eyes. "It's scientifically proven." There's a catch in the last word, as if the effort of being even slightly funny is too much.

Cattarina comes out from under the bed and stands a few feet away. Maybe she senses his distress.

"Look at that," he says. "I might be winning her over."

"You might."

He heads into the bathroom. I toss my yogurt container and bend to pet Cattarina. "You should be friendly with Dalton. He's one of the good ones."

She lifts her nose so I can scratch under her chin. "I'll be back in a while."

The day is bright and sunshiny. My ponytail swishes against my back as I take off down the street. I planned to listen to an audiobook, but there are so many people about, watering grass, walking their dogs, and being friendly that I decide to live in the moment, waving and saying hello.

I reach a pocket park and cut across it, enjoying the trees and the squeak of playground equipment, empty at this hour but shifting in the breeze.

About two-thirds of the way through the park, at a cluster of scraggly bushes, I hear a strange sound. Something about it makes me stop instantly.

Is that a kid crying? I look around. The swings and slide are unoccupied. There's nobody in my immediate vicinity.

I stay still, listening.

Then I hear it again. Was it a cat?

The trees rustle overhead, and I look up. There's nothing I can see. No stranded kitty. I walk among the trunks, staring into the branches.

Then I hear it again, low, not high. It's on the ground.

There must be a cat in this thatch of brush.

I walk around it. There are ten or so bushes growing wild in a dip in the ground. Along the edge are piles of trapped leaves and other debris that blew through the park and got stuck in the low limbs.

I peer into the thicket, but I can't see anything.

The sound comes again, more plaintive this time, as if this cat knows I'm close.

Is it lost? Hurt? Maybe it will have tags or a chip. I can take it to a veterinarian and they can scan it.

If it will let me catch it.

Or it could be a stray.

When I worked at the rescue, we got cats in all sorts of situations. Lost, abandoned, or just plain born into street life. I'm not sure about the networks here in LA, but I bet there are a lot. Animal lovers are everywhere.

I fostered several kitten litters in the summers I was in grad school, when my course load was light and I could manage them. They take an incredible amount of care.

But one stray cat is easy.

Catching it, not so much.

I think I spot a movement deep in the bushes. I get down on my knees and begin parting the leaves.

I know I'm close when I hear a faint hiss.

"It's okay, sweet baby," I say. "You're all right."

Sticks catch in my hair as I crawl deeper into the bramble. My arms get scratched, but I persist. If the cat isn't running, it might be hurt.

There's space low to the ground beneath the biggest bushes. The earth gets damp, which is probably why they grow so well.

Then I spot two gleaming eyes. The cat is young, not even a year old. Her back is to me, showing off pretty gray stripes along her coal black fur. Her head twists to watch me warily.

"Hey," I say. "Will you come with me?" I wish I had treats or any kind of food, but naturally I left with only my phone. I wasn't expecting a kitty rescue. I reach out and stroke the matted fur.

My heart catches at how thin this sweet cat is. Her eyes close for a minute. She's breathing shallowly, like it's hard.

Then I hear a soft mew.

Wait. That wasn't her. I was watching.

Then another.

Oh, no. Are there kittens?

I keep petting her softly. I can't get any closer with my head due to how thick the branches are. But I reach with my hand over her belly to the other side.

I feel a tiny head. Then another. Then another.

It's a litter.

"Poor baby! You're just a baby yourself!"

I snag one of the kittens and carefully lift it to the mother cat's back to assess its age. The mother drops her head to her paws, as if she doesn't have the energy to fight me over taking one.

The kitten's eyes are open, but it's undersized. Four weeks, I'd guess, even though it's so light that it feels like a bundle of feathers.

I set it back down. These kittens won't survive much longer. The mother is not well.

I press my hand to her belly. Her respiration is labored and fast. I feel around her neck. No collar or any impression that there ever was one. She is a stray that got pregnant the moment she matured. Kittens can go into their first heat at four or five months old.

Good gracious.

How do I get them out?

I crawl backward out of the bushes. I'm not far from home, but I can't carry a litter of kittens in my arms. I need something.

The park is empty this early. A lone jogger passes through the center.

What do I do?

Tears smart in my eyes. I could run home and get Cattarina's crate. I keep it in the back of my Jeep. Then I could take them to a vet.

Except it's Saturday. Only the emergency care would be open.

I can call them. Or a rescue. That would be better.

But I have to get them out of the bushes. Something tells me this is urgent for the mother.

I head back through the park to go home, but then I spot a trash can spilling over. Beside it is a box!

My feet push into a jog. The box is mostly empty, a bit of extra trash in it. I smoosh the trash down into the bin and take the box. I'll carry them home in this. Then I can stabilize them while I call around.

Now to get them out.

I walk to the bushes again and find another way with more space between the ground and lower branches. I set the box beside me and army-crawl in the dirt.

I'm approaching the kitten side this time, and I count four. Mama's head is down. She doesn't even bother to hiss.

I can only use one hand to get a kitten, as I need the other to push my way out again, but I get the first one into the box.

Then I'm back in. I hold two of them together. They are so small and weak.

I pause for a second as I place them in the box. Prepare yourself, Nadia. It's possible they won't make it. Be ready.

My lips press together as I go back in for the fourth kitten. The mother cat seems to realize that I've taken them and lifts her head to hiss at me again.

"I've got you, Mama," I tell her. "Don't worry."

I move the last kitten to the box. Now for the hard part. She might get a spike of energy when I try to move her. Or if she's hurt, that could make her fight.

I go back in. "Please don't bite me," I tell her. "I'm trying to help."

When I'm close to her again, I stroke her fur. "We're

going to do this together, okay, Mama? We'll get you back with your kittens."

The back of my hand slides through mud and gunk as it moves beneath her. This is gross.

But she doesn't protest. I move my other hand beneath her head. She's so weak. I pull her close to my chest so I can hold her in place as I crawl backward.

I'm sure I look ridiculous coming out from beneath the bushes, my knees, shirt, and elbows covered in mud, twigs in my hair, and a scrawny pile of matted fur in my arms.

But I get her out.

The kittens are balled together, two of them mewing pitifully. The others seem too weak to even cry.

I set the mother next to them and arrange them snugly together.

Now to get them home.

I walk as quickly as I can without jostling them. When I reach our parking lot, I go even faster. The mother cat seems to stare into nothingness and I'm afraid that the act of moving her was already too much.

A sob catches in my throat as I madly burst through the door of the apartment and flip on the lights.

I've forgotten about Dalton. He's on the bed, the blackout curtains drawn. "What's going on?" he asks.

"I think she died on the way here!" I cry, setting the box on the carpet and falling to my knees.

Dalton scrambles out of the bed. "Who?"

"Mama cat!" I lift her from the box. She's listless and unmoving. "Oh, no!"

I curl her into my body, trying to feel to see if she's breathing or if she has a heartbeat. "I have to help her!"

Dalton kneels next to me. "Set her on the carpet."

"Can you help her?"

"I'm not a veterinarian, but I'll try. Do you have something that can hydrate her? Like a medicine plunger or turkey baster?"

"I have a liquid syringe from the cold medicine."

"Make sure it's clean and bring it with some water."

I race to the kitchen to gather those things. When I come back, Dalton is pressing fingers against her chest. "Okay, she has a heartbeat. Give me the water."

He draws some water into the plunger and carefully puts it in her mouth. "Mix some of Cattarina's wet food with water to make a thin paste and get a towel."

I hurry to get those as well.

When I return, he's massaging her chest and body. "Come on, kitty. Take in some water." He gives her more.

"Should I wrap her in the towel?"

"Yes. The idea is to make her body have to do as little as possible. It's what we do to humans."

He takes the watered-down paste and draws some into the syringe. "You look after the kittens. We need to warm up the towels."

"I have the heating pad I used with the rescues."

"Perfect."

I drag one of my suitcases out, glad I held on to a few things from my rescue days. I find the heating pad and a small circular lamb's wool cushion I would put on top of it.

I plug it into the wall near the box.

"Is she responding?" I ask, crawling back to the mother cat.

Dalton cradles her body wrapped in the towel. "She swallowed. That's a good sign. We'll warm her up and see if she'll respond. We'll need to get her to a vet."

"I'll start calling."

I drag my phone out of the pocket of my shorts and start Googling emergency vets.

"There she goes," Dalton says, and I look up.

Mama cat licks the end of the syringe. He squirts out a little more.

"That's the biggest hurdle," he says. "Stabilizing them for the next step."

"Same as cats as in humans?"

He nods. "She's coming around." He holds on to her and peers into the box. "When I think I can set her down, I'll look at the others, but they are all wiggling."

I place the first call, then move the box closer to the wall socket so I can slide the warming cushion beneath the litter. They all look up at me and cry with faint mews. They're all mewing. My eyes smart with tears.

A voice comes on the line. "SoCal Emergency Pet Care, how can I help you?"

As I explain the situation to the woman, I glance up at Dalton. He's watching the mother cat as he slowly feeds her watered-down food. He's so intent on her, as if saving her can somehow make this hard day better than it was.

And my heart definitely catches at the sight.

18

DALTON

Nadia insisted she could manage the cats at the emergency clinic and there was no point for me to lose my sleep between shifts sitting in a waiting room.

I reluctantly let her go and fall asleep instantly, waking only when I hear the door open.

"How are they?" I ask.

She rests a cat crate on the floor. "Discharged. Mom is eating. Kittens were fed. They all got flea baths. I have some nutrition supplements and kitten formula to take the load off Mama Cat while she recovers."

"So they came home?" I sit up and rub my head.

"Yes. I couldn't afford to leave them, and they didn't think it would matter as long as they were monitored."

"Did you find a rescue?"

She unlatches the top of the cage and pulls it off. "Every one of them I called was full. I'm on several waiting lists."

"I wonder if anyone ever gets off the list."

She shrugs. "There are lots of homeless cats in the world."

I kneel in front of the crate, half-asleep even though Nadia was gone for a solid five hours. "So now we have more secret cats?"

"Are you upset?" Her voice has a note of panic in it, as if she believes I might kick the litter out.

"No. Just wonder how Cattarina is going to handle it."

"She loves other cats, usually. It's her size that scares them." Nadia bites her lip, her eyes shifting to the bed. "She'll come out eventually and investigate."

We sit opposite each other on the floor, the crate between us. All the cats are asleep. I reach to pet the mother, her fur soft from the flea baths. They all look like fluff balls.

"Should we name them?" I ask her. "Or is that a bad idea with rescues that might get adopted?"

"Of course we should." She reaches in to run a thumb over the top of the first one's head. He's solid gray with white feet. "Greyson," she says.

"Fitting."

She touches the second, an orange one. "Pumpkin."

"Easy to remember."

"You do the next two," she says.

I slide my finger down the short tail of a black one. It looks exactly like its mother. "Doppelgänger."

"That's a mouthful."

"But so many nicknames. Dop. BopDop. Boppy. Boppadeedop."

She laughs. "Okay."

The fourth one stirs, lifting its head. It's stark white with no other color. It mews at us. "Ferris Mewler," I say. "Ferris, for short. Or Save Ferris. Or just Mew."

She laughs again. "You make it so complicated."

"What about Mama Cat? The original MC? MC Catter? Can't Touch This?"

Now Nadia is in giggles, and the sound is so pure, so happy, that the day is completely turned around from the terrible hospital shift.

Something brushes against my elbow. I jerk my arm up, then realize Cattarina has come out from under the bed. "We have visitors," I tell her.

Nadia quiets, watching her cat approach the crate. She sniffs the edges, then pokes her face over the top. She's big enough that she can see over it without lifting her body.

Ferris Mewler spots her and wiggles to the edge, almost as if he thinks this is another source of milk.

Cattarina strains over the side, her face nearing the uplifted head of the kitten.

The two of them touch noses, then Cattarina moves fast, grabbing the kitten by the scruff. Before we can even react, she's dashed to the bed and leaped on top with the kitten.

"Cattarina!" Nadia cries, jumping to her feet.

By the time we catch up to the cats, Cattarina has Ferris curled into her belly and is licking his head.

"What should we do?" Nadia asks. "Take the kitten away?"

I turn back to the crate. "I'm not taking anything from your cat. She might eat me. Besides, we should think about sleeping arrangements. Does Cattarina have a bed?"

"Yes, under ours. I keep it hidden because she won't sleep on it out here."

I kneel by the bed and push the suitcases aside.

"It's toward the back, near the corner," Nadia says.

I grasp the corner of the pale blue bed and drag it out. "If that's her sleeping spot, she'll take the kittens down there and it will be hard to get them," I say.

"I'm sure you're right." Nadia's eyebrows knit together in concern. "We need to make it accessible if she's going to steal them."

"Hopefully Mama Cat won't fight her for them." I glance around. "We have to kitten proof this place. Those babies are going to be everywhere as soon as they get stronger."

"We're going to need a bigger litter box," Nadia quips, and I laugh out loud.

"We are."

Nadia gives the other kittens one more pat, then heads across the room to the bed. "Cattarina, you can't steal MC's babies."

As if to counter Nadia's words, Cattarina places her paw protectively over Ferris.

"Come on," Nadia says. "Let's get on your bed, and you can keep the kitten for a while." She reaches in and takes the kitten. "Come on."

"Where should this go?" I ask, sliding the large cat bed across the floor.

Nadia blows out a gush of air. "Maybe between the

sofa and the wall? That feels protected without being too hard for us to reach."

I nod and set the bed in the corner. Then I back away.

"Come along, little Ferris," Nadia says, carrying the baby to the big bed. "Maybe you can convince Cattarina to sleep out in the room."

The moment the kitten is left alone, Cattarina leaps across the floor. But she approaches the bed tentatively.

"Let's see what she does," Nadia says. "Hopefully, she'll accept being out here."

Cattarina places one paw into her bed, leaning down to nose the kitten, who has fallen asleep. She curls around it.

"Look at that," Nadia whispers. "It worked." She looks up at me with the happiest expression I've ever seen on her. My belly warms over. I want her to always be this happy.

"Looks like you're a cat mom six times over," I tell her.

She points at where my hand has mindlessly returned to the box of cats to stroke them one by one. "And you're a cat dad."

What is happening here? I've never had one pet, much less half a dozen. But as Nadia and I take kittens out one at a time to feed them, then take the mama cat aside so she can eat in peace to regain her strength, I realize—I like it.

Now it feels even more like home, the sort of home I've never known before now.

19

NADIA

Four kittens, a weak mama cat, and a thieving Catzilla are a lot of work.

When Dalton leaves for his shift that evening, I'm tasked with feeding four kittens, teaching them to use the litter box, and continually bringing them back to their mother when Cattarina the Great steals them for her own bed.

By two a.m., I'm exhausted. I lie on the bed, barely registering when Cattarina jumps up beside me. She rarely does that, but I'm too tired to figure out why.

When Dalton comes in the next morning, he tries to be quiet, but the mere arrival of sunlight in the room wakes up me, Cattarina, and the kittens, and the mewling begins.

I sit up, trying to push my wild hair into some semblance of order. "Shift go okay?"

"Easy one. How was the first night as a mother of six?"

"Exhausting."

He chuckles, and the sound makes me smile despite my tiredness. "You go back to sleep. I'll handle a round."

"I don't think I'll sleep."

He turns on the kitchen light. "We have two kittens in the crate. Mama Cat in Cattarina's bed. And we're missing a big cat and two babies."

I shift my pillow to reveal the oversized Maine Coon and two kittens.

"I see." He leans beside me to scoop up the two kittens. "I'll borrow these." I catch a whiff of him while he's close. There's a hospital smell, for sure, one I've gotten used to, something antiseptic. But also a quality that is always his, clean cotton clothes and a hint of herbal shampoo.

Cattarina glares at him as he takes the kittens away. I stroke her head. "They'll be fine, Cattarina. Let Dad feed them."

Just saying the word *Dad* does something weird in my belly. It's awfully domestic, even more than the meals and the shared space. We have responsibility now.

And Dalton's doing his share, despite his difficult schedule.

He returns the kittens to the crate with the others, then turns on the burner under the pot of water we use to warm up the kitten formula. "How is Mama Cat?"

"Sleeping, mostly, but it looks like a comfortable rest."

"That will do her the most good. Sleep in a safe, warm place, food, someone to help with the babies."

I join him by the stove. "I'm supposed to go to work today. Should I take off?"

"I can feed them."

"But you need to sleep."

"I have twenty-four hours off. Plenty of time to watch them. You'll be home late afternoon?"

"Yes."

"I'll sleep then."

I turn to look over the room. Cattarina is sneaking toward the crate to steal a kitten. "I'm hoping they'll be more independent when Mama is better."

He checks the temperature of the formula. "I'll look her over when she wakes. I think she'll perk up quickly."

I head to the shower to get ready for work. I feel bad that I've soaked up all of Dalton's free time between shifts.

But when I come out in my jeans and deli shirt, he's got my yogurt out, coffee made, and two kittens on his lap.

I think he likes it.

I'm not quiet coming in after my workday. Dalton said he would sleep when I got home. I'm anxious to see how Mama Cat is doing.

But when I step inside the apartment, the side with the bed is dark from the blackout curtains.

The kitchen bulb is on, just enough light to see on the sofa side.

I check Cattarina's bed in its new placement.

Empty.

I peer into the open crate.

Nothing.

Where is everyone?

I stand still. There's no sound. Did he take them somewhere? Did Mama Cat take a turn for the worse?

Surely he would have messaged me if there was a problem.

I set my bag on the bar and peer into the gloom of the bed.

There's a figure there. Dalton must be asleep. But where are the cats?

My heart hammers as I turn on the flashlight function of my phone and angle it so that it doesn't shine directly on the bed. Maybe Cattarina hauled everyone under the bed and Mama Cat followed?

I'm about to kneel to look below when I hear a meow near my face.

It can't be Cattarina. She's silent. And it's too big of a sound for the kittens.

I carefully angle the phone at the wall to give a bit of reflected light on the bed.

Dalton is curled in a semi-circle around the whole pile of fur. Cattarina is closest to his belly, her head up, eyes alert.

Mama Cat is next, watching me. She meows again.

I reach out to pet her head. She must be feeling better.

The kittens are a writhing mass along her belly. They are probably nursing. I need to feed them before they drain all of MC's energy.

The glow of the light illuminates Dalton's face, or half of it. He's partially buried in his pillow.

His features are soft and gentle. His breathing is regular and deep.

My chest warms over. He's beautiful with his thick eyebrows and angled nose. His sharp jawline is shadowed with a hint of facial hair.

He draws in a jagged breath, different from his previous calm rhythm. The older cats' faces snap to me in judgment, as if I'm guilty of waking him.

I angle the phone light down to the floor, leaving him in darkness. "Sorry," I whisper.

I tiptoe to the kitchen to warm up formula for the kittens so they won't overtax their mother. Then I carefully take them one by one to the sofa to feed them.

Dalton sleeps on. I wonder if he arranged the cats near him, or if he fell asleep and they gathered there.

My question is answered when I pause in feeding the kitten to examine the bottle.

Cattarina jumps from the bed and darts to the sofa. She snatches the kitten from my lap and carries her back to her mother.

I get it.

It's not only the cats who are a family.

It's all of us.

20

DALTON

I wake up to a tickle on my cheek.

Must be one of the cats.

It's dim, but I can tell from the light leaking below the blackout curtains that it's morning. I'll have to go to work soon.

I reach out to figure out which cat is in my face, but I touch a face instead.

Nadia?

I reach behind me to adjust the curtain enough that a crack of light comes through.

Yeah, it's her. The cats are in between us, surrounded by the circle made by Nadia's body and mine.

The cats are all asleep. Cattarina, who was against my belly last I checked, has moved up against Nadia. Mama Cat is curled against me.

The four kittens are in the middle.

When did Nadia get in bed?

And how am I going to get out?

I lie there a while longer, taking in the situation. It's nice. The whole mixed-up family, all together in one bed.

I remember our conversation over apple pie, before the cats arrived. Both of us felt a spark. She wanted to know what it meant.

It's grown. I can feel it. Can she feel it, too? It's a glow, maybe even a flame.

And she's right here in bed with me.

Of course, so are the cats.

She must have been too tired to blow up the mattress. I peer beyond her to the floor. No, it's there, her blue ruffled comforter on top.

Huh. Now I'm really curious.

My side of the bed is against the wall, the window directly above. I can wriggle to the end of it, where there is a small amount of space before you get to the dresser.

But the moment I start moving downward, I realize I'm trapped beneath the sheet. The cats are lying on it, and so is Nadia.

I glance at the clock. An hour until my shift starts. Not much time to dally.

I reach behind me to find the edge of the sheet. I need to pull it off me, get my legs out, and then I can scoot down the bed.

But the minute I tug on it, Mama Cat stirs. And once she moves, the kittens squirm toward her. I can't let them nurse long. We need to supplement until Mama is better.

I lift the first kitten to take her away to feed her and try to inch my way off the bed using my elbows.

But now more kittens are up, and the mewling begins.

Too late.

Nadia stirs. "Hey," she says.

I pause in my reverse Army crawl off the bed. "Hey."

"Sorry if I crowded you," she says. "The kittens kept squirming off the bed and almost falling. I moved them all to the crate after I fed them, but Cattarina brought them back up here. It was a losing battle." She yawns into her hand.

"Yeah, I gave up, too. So you came up here to keep them from falling off?"

She nods. "I wasn't getting any sleep on the air mattress, worried about them."

"I'm glad you came up here."

Her gaze meets mine. We lock for a second, the intimacy of the moment like a ribbon winding around us.

Yeah, something is definitely happening.

"Dalton?"

Is she going to admit it, too?

My throat is thick as I say, "Yeah?"

"Do you think we'll have to keep sleeping like this?" She scrunches her nose like it's not a good idea.

Disappointment washes over me. "Maybe we could roll up a blanket to keep them from wriggling off."

But her frown deepens. Did I read this wrong? Does she *want* to be in the bed with all of us?

"If we have to do it like this, it's fine by me," she says.

So she does.

Our gazes clash again. Something's happening here. The air is charged. I'm too far away to lean in, trapped by the sheet and besides, there's a whole litter between us.

But she watches me, and it happens again, her gaze dropping to my lips.

This is going to happen.

I'm going to make it happen.

She breaks the spell by pushing the sheet away. "I'm going to take off today since we'll both be gone. Mondays are slow anyway. Is this a twelve or twenty-hour shift for you?"

It's like the moment never happened.

"Twelve," I say.

"So we'll both be back here tonight."

"Sounds like it." What is she suggesting?

"I guess we'll all sleep together again."

My throat tightens. Nadia and me. In the bed. On purpose.

"I don't think it will be too long that we have to fight this," she says. "The kittens will get strong enough to climb down without getting hurt."

"They will."

She slides backward off the bed. "I'll get started feeding them."

I watch her walk through the semi-dark to the kitchen to warm the formula. She moves with grace, even at this early hour, her legs pale beneath pajama shorts. The top hugs her chest, and my body starts reacting.

Down, boy.

Good thing we have a whole bevy of felines in between us. Because in this cozy half-dark room after sleeping in the same bed, she is too temptingly close to resist.

Fitz and Harrington wait for me when I arrive in the locker room. Fitz wears a surgery cap over her springy curls, and I'm immediately jealous. She got a plum job to start off, clearly.

Harrington tugs off his Mr. Rogers-styled cardigan and holds it in front of his chest.

"What?" I ask as I open my locker.

"We need an update about the roommate," Fitz says. "Now that you're co-parenting."

"How's all the pussy action?" Harrington asks, but with no swagger, and a giggle at the end that makes him seem like a teen boy.

I drag my lanyard with my ID over my head. "Kittens are healthy. Mama cat is stable."

Fitz leans against my locker. "You know what we mean. Is it getting cozy now that you have a whole family?" Her grin is so wide that dimples are revealed. She reminds me of Geena Davis in *Thelma and Louise*, my mom's favorite movie.

"It's different," I say, slamming my locker and heading for coffee before I have to check in.

Fitz follows me and Harrington hurriedly shoves his cardigan in his locker so he can catch up.

"What do you mean, different?" Fitz asks as we dodge a rolling gurney pushed by two orderlies.

"She slept on the bed last night," I say.

"With you?" Fitz's mouth forms an "O" of surprise.

"And all the cats." We reach the coffee cart, and I pay for a drip with a shot of espresso. The woman knows my usual order and hands me the cup.

The others wait, already holding their first round of caffeine. It's how we start all our morning shifts.

"So no love connection," Harrington says.

I turn and head for the ER. "Nope. So what's with the surgical gear?" I ask Fitz.

This gets her going. As we walk the halls, she regales us with every detail of how our attending is allowing her to assist on a surgery for a case she had last shift.

"Lucky," Harrington says as we approach Booker, who is waiting to give us assignments.

Fitz peels off to head for surgery.

"And I guess we're covering for her," Harrington says.

"Some people have all the fun," I say, ready for Booker's scowl and the first cases of the day.

"Your fun happens at home," Harrington says.

Booker turns to us. "You're late. Harrington, to orthopedics." She glares at me a moment, peering at my face. "Murphy, wipe that smile off your face. There's a man with swollen testicles with your name on it."

"On it." But even as I head to the curtained ER, none of them can really bring me down.

I am smiling.

And I'm definitely looking forward to tonight.

21

NADIA

I find myself anticipating Dalton's arrival that night more than I should.

I don't know what it is. Maybe the coziness of the cat family. The ups and downs of caring for them. His willingness to help.

Or how we ended up in the same bed.

Is this the way my mom feels about Dad coming home? I can almost juxtapose her happy expression on my face.

It feels the same.

Is this a bad thing?

We do live together. He's kind of … great. And we noticed each other from the very start.

Maybe it's inevitable.

I've spent the last half-hour picking up kittens and setting them back in the crate. Maybe we should get a taller box. They are not litter box trained yet. Mama Cat isn't quite up to the task of cleaning them up, and I really don't want formula poop all over the apartment.

Mama Cat and Catzilla are asleep on the bed—mine, not theirs. Their kitty pad is empty in the corner.

The kittens are awake and feisty after being fed.

Ferris Mewler uses Pumpkin as a stepping stool to grasp the top edge of the crate. Then he's over the top, belly caught on the lip, front paws outstretched as if he can touch the ground.

I pick him up and set him back inside.

But then it's Greyson who straight up launches himself over the top. I catch him with both hands, my palms stinging from tiny baby cat claws.

"Back in you go."

Greyson mews at me, probably using some kitten-curse words.

The lock jiggles as Dalton inserts his key. I know that sound well by now. So do the cats, as they look up at the door expectantly.

I inhale sharply as my anticipation peaks. My heart actually *leaps*.

Should it be doing that?

It doesn't matter.

It's doing it whether or not it should.

The aroma of hot pizza reaches me before I see his face.

He's brought dinner?

The door opens only a crack. "Is it safe to avoid escaping cats?" he calls.

Greyson is sneaking over the wall of the crate. I lift him off and set him next to his siblings. "All clear!"

Dalton enters quickly, holding the pizza box over his head as if the cats could reach it.

The smell does something to them. Mama Cat abandons the bed to weave between Dalton's legs.

Catzilla hops down after her to sit at his feet.

"Apparently our kitties like pizza," I tell him.

"I see that." He steps carefully across the floor, trying to avoid errant paws. Both cats follow closely.

"You stopped for food?"

"I thought it would be too crazy to cook. And if you had, we would have something to heat another time."

My chest flutters like someone blew a dandelion inside of it. He thought of us, of me. "I haven't had a moment to cook at all."

"Then we can eat it hot." He sets the box on the bar and the two older cats immediately hop up to investigate.

"Cattarina!" I cry, standing to pull her down.

Dalton laughs. "She's motivated." He picks up Mama cat. "Or maybe MC Catter, Can't Touch This, is a bad influence." He lifts the kitty to his nose. "Are you, now?" He sets her on his shoulder and strokes her back. "So skinny."

"That will take some time, especially if she keeps letting the babies nurse." Both Greyson and Ferris have escaped the crate. They are getting too strong to stop, recovering much faster than their mother.

"Into the litter box," I tell them, lifting both and scooting toward the bar. I set them both inside, letting them sniff so they start to understand what happens there.

Greyson already gets it, letting a stream of pee fly into the litter.

Ferris takes a bite.

"Ferris!" I lift him out and clear out his mouth. "That's for pooping, not eating!"

Dalton laughs. "They'll figure it out."

"Greyson just peed in there!"

Mama Cat jumps back to the bar, and Dalton moves her down again. "She's obviously getting her energy back."

"She needs to take over her brood." I snag her and put her in the litter box with Ferris. "Don't let your kid eat the rocks."

Ferris noses the litter again.

Mama Cat whacks him on the head with her paw.

"Tough love," Dalton says with a laugh.

The two exit the litter box, followed by Greyson, who seems pretty pleased with himself, holding up his head as he crosses the floor.

Dalton bends down and extends a hand to me. "Your dinner, Madame?"

I take his fingers, that spark I felt a few days ago returning, becoming a buzz that sizzles through my whole body.

He lifts me up from the floor. "Should we get plates or eat it straight from the box like new parents who don't have time for dishes?"

"Straight from the box. I'm too tired for anything else."

"Done."

We head into the kitchen to wash our hands. It's strangely intimate, taking turns soaping up and rinsing off, passing the same kitchen towel between us. It's nothing like showering together, but something about it feels the same.

"You sit. I'll get us water," he says.

"Was your shift okay?" I ask. "You must be tired."

"Not too bad. I might be getting used to it." He removes two cups from the cabinet.

I open the pizza box, drawing both cats onto the bar again.

"Goodness, kitties," I say, setting them both down. "No, no."

When Catzilla crouches like she might jump again, I hold a hand in front of her face. "No, Cattarina. No, no."

She narrows her eyes at me, then turns and heads to the bed, jumping up to glare from a distance.

Mama Cat looks between Cattarina and me, then hops into the crate where Doppelgänger and Pumpkin are mewing like they're all alone in the world.

"Now we can eat," Dalton says, setting our cups down.

The pizza is half meat lover's, half veggie. Opposites, sharing a space.

He remembers my order like I do his.

Six weeks of living together, and we know each other.

Except what it feels like to touch him. To kiss that mouth.

I focus on my slice of pizza to scatter those wild thoughts, the peppers and mushrooms threatening to slide off as if giving chase to my far-flung feelings.

We tuck into the warm and savory food, each taking

turns glancing back at the room to see what the cats are up to.

MC settles in with her two.

Cattarina fetches Ferris and Greyson, the wildlings, and brings them onto the mattress with her.

"So much for the cat bed," Dalton says, reaching for a second slice. "Are we going to make the parental circle of protection around them again tonight?"

I realized earlier that with the bed against the wall, I could sleep with them on the inside, and the kittens weren't in danger of falling.

But I simply say, "I guess so."

I don't miss how he swallows hard, even though he hadn't taken a bite. He's thinking about it, all of us in the bed.

I am, too.

We finish half the pizza and put the rest away, then warm a round of kitten formula and each take two kittens to feed. Soon, we won't need this routine. The kittens can start solid foods now that they aren't so weak. Then Mama Cat can really recover.

They're going to be fine.

Dalton showers as I pick up the formula from the feeding. When he comes out, I go in, deciding a quick shower would be good for me, too, since we will be in such close proximity.

The room smells of him. The herbal shampoo, a woodsy body wash. I close my eyes, letting the water wash over me, cocooned in the warmth of where he just was.

Naked.

And now I'm here.

Naked.

An ache spreads through me. I haven't dated anyone seriously in two years. I had a boyfriend in college. When I graduated and left to get my MBA, we tried staying together as a long-distance relationship.

But the time apart revealed how little we had in common when we couldn't Netflix and chill the night away. Our phone conversations became texts. Then those became fewer. We didn't break up so much as stop talking, until one day he said it seemed like we were done, and I agreed.

Not bad, as far as endings go.

We haven't talked since, although every once in a while I feel this twinge of having known someone so well, so intimately, and now I don't know them at all. I couldn't tell you where he lives. What he's doing.

I don't remember what he puts on pizza.

I've dallied longer than I intended. Dalton may already be asleep.

For some reason, this upsets me, so I hurriedly turn off the water and towel dry.

I had pinned my hair up rather than wash it, but I let it fall, soft and damp on the edges. I brush my teeth, wondering if he's awake. If he's anticipating me sleeping on the bed with him.

Or if the darn cats have finally decided to curl up in their own bed and I'm not needed.

That would suck.

I shouldn't have worried on any count. When I leave the bathroom, the small kitchen light is on, but the rest of the room is bathed in darkness. It's been a good compromise since we have been getting up to feed the kittens.

I can see the form of Dalton on the bed. I peer into the crate.

His voice is low. "They're all up here. Ferris has already tried to tumble off twice."

My belly quivers as I approach the bed. "Ferris is the wiliest of them all."

"I concur."

My eyes adjust. Dalton lies against the wall, all six cats dead center on the bed.

"I can be on the edge," he says.

"I like it over here."

"Then we officially have sides," he says.

"We do." I shiver lightly with another couple-oriented detail now solidified between us.

Both of our comforters are on the bed, his Trans-formers one covering him, and my blue one on the open side.

Sliding beneath the sheet is wildly intimate. Even with the cats between us, and no clear path from my body to his, it's unabashedly sexy to slip into bed beside him.

"I'll take first shift if they wake up hungry," he says.

"I'll get up, too. It'll go faster."

"All right."

His voice reverberates through me in the dark. It's low and sexy, like an audiobook narrator.

Which makes me think of romance novels. Then *First Base to Love*. Then *cock*.

I don't think I'll sleep, but then my eyes pop open in the dark.

Something feels different.

The kitchen bulb is on, leaving a soft glow over the room. I hold my breath, listening. No mewling or cries from the kittens.

I've rolled onto my side, facing away from Dalton and the cats. I turn slowly, ever so carefully, to look at them.

They're not there. The space between us is empty.

I sit up. Where are they?

Dalton stirs. "Everything okay?"

"The cats are gone."

He looks down. "They moved."

I slide out from under the covers. "Let me look."

But I needn't have worried. The whole lot of them are in the cat bed.

Catzilla opens one eye, then closes it again.

I tiptoe back to Dalton. "Maybe we were too restless."

"Maybe."

I've already slid back under the covers when I realize I don't need to. There are no kittens to keep from falling off.

I'll have to blow up the air mattress. I'm about to leave again when Dalton says, "I checked the lease."

I stay put. "Really?"

"Two pet maximum."

"Uh oh."

He sighs. "I guess we'll have to keep quiet about the cats."

"We will."

"And hope they don't need anything in here."

I grip the comforter. "Would they evict us?"

"I'm not sure. They'd probably give us a few days to re-home them."

But where would I do that? The rescues are full. Camryn couldn't handle the whole litter with her allergies. I don't know very many people in LA.

My breath hitches.

Dalton's arm crosses the bed to brush against my shoulder. "Hey. We'll figure it out. So far, so good."

His touch sets off another jolt, like the one we talked about a week ago.

I shouldn't bring it up. Not here. At night. Both of us are in bed.

But I do. "I felt that," I say.

"Me, too." His voice has that low, sexy quality again.

His hand stays on my shoulder, heavy and warm. I never want him to move it. A shower of sparks courses through me every time I breathe, shifting my body just enough that the contact changes. Each tiny alteration in pressure, every bare increment of skin newly touched, is like a flame making its way across me.

I've never been so sensitive to something. Dopamine and oxytocin. They're working overtime.

"Will it fade?" I ask. "It seems like it's growing more intense."

"Do you want it to go away?"

His question is simple, and so is my answer.

"No."

His eyes catch the faint light of the kitchen bulb. His

face is shadowy but so familiar. I can picture the cut of his jaw, the breadth of his brow, the angle of his nose.

"Nadia?"

My name is like a question in the dark.

"Yes?"

He says nothing in response, as if his next words are too big, too much. I wonder how he'd phrase it. Would he ask me to move closer? To kiss me? If this is a good idea?

If he should leave the bed?

Suddenly I can't bear that possibility. I don't want him to go. I don't want to go either.

So I take a leap.

And I move closer.

22

DALTON

When Nadia scoots closer to me, I decide not to risk any questions. I think she already answered it, anyway.

I should stay here.

With her.

My hand glides under her neck. She's close, even though it's hard to make her out in the dark.

Still, with my hand beneath her head, I know where her lips are. I lean over her, and the gentle press of my mouth to hers is a revelation, a shower of sparks and lightning bolts and the softness of her kiss.

I keep it there a moment, letting the rush settle so that I can feel her without the distraction of the shock that we've come here. To take my time, acting with thoughtfulness and care.

Nadia's hand moves to my shoulder. Her touch on me kicks off another cascade of intense need, making my vision splotchy behind my lids.

I wonder for a moment why the hormones are

flooding so hard with her, more than I've ever experienced. But then I simply let them wash over me, and deepen the kiss, learning the taste of her in the night, faintly of toothpaste, but also some basic essence that is all her, the sum of all the sensory data I've learned in the nearly two months we've lived together.

I want to touch her, all of her, and it takes conscious effort to wrestle control. Instead, I knead the back of her neck, feeling her muscles relax in my hand, her hair slipping through my fingers.

All the desire for her, starting from that first meeting under the stairs of a courtyard, has built to this moment. I tighten my grip on her, and she does the same on my shoulder. The kiss grows more frantic, our tongues meeting, exploring.

My erection presses painfully against the elastic band of my shorts, and I shift to move it aside.

Nadia moves with me, her body sliding more fully beneath me, so that when I return to my position, my hips press into her belly.

She sucks in a breath, feeling me hard against her. I slow down the kiss, waiting to see what she will do. Is this where she will stomp the brakes? It's not a bad idea, take our time…

But her body arches to meet mine, increasing the pressure of me against her. My brain whites out a moment, and whatever hesitation I felt disappears into the crash of need.

I leave her lips, pressing my mouth against her jaw, her throat, and finding the slender strap of her pajama top. I release her neck to grasp the bit of fabric and tug it down, tasting the skin of her collarbone and following the line across her shoulder.

She arches again, and I know where she wants me to go. I take my time, easing the shirt down, letting it catch on her nipple.

Then, with a sharp tug, I expose the breast and cover it with my mouth.

She draws in a quick breath, her hand moving to the back of my head to keep me in place.

I'm not leaving anytime soon. Her body is soft and pliable. I encircle the breast and cup it fully, sucking on the tight peak.

She lets out a small cry, wriggling beneath me, pressing upward with her hips to feel me against her.

I'm overcome with another rush and grasp the other breast, sliding over her body more fully to control where my dick slides against her, aiming lower so that I grind between her thighs.

She cries out again, her hands moving to my waist, guiding my body where she wants the pressure. Her body quivers, and I know the tidal wave of chemistry has taken over her, too.

"Dalton," she breathes, and she doesn't have to say anything else. I know what she's after.

I slip a hand inside her pajama shorts and beneath the silky panties below. She's hot and wet, and slipping fingers inside her is like touching something divine.

She clutches my shoulders. She's gorgeously responsive, moving with me, telegraphing what she wants, and I give it to her, plunging inside and tweaking the swollen bud of her clit.

"Dalton, Dalton, Dalton, Dalton." My name on her lips makes me twitch with every repetition. I want inside her, buried in her body, fucking her until she no longer remembers my name.

I return my mouth to her breast, grazing her nipple with my teeth. Her back arches to me, her hips moving rhythmically with every stroke of my fingers inside her.

She's wet and slick and I revel in every texture, every sound, every twitch of her body. Her breathing speeds up, and I can feel the rapid firing of her heart beneath my cheek.

I pull away to look at her face, wanting to see what this does to her, even in the shadow of the near-dark.

Nadia's eyes are squeezed shut, her eyebrows drawn together. She sucks in a breath, her white teeth flash, catching the dim light of the kitchen lamp.

Then she tightens around my fingers. Her core muscles contract against my side where we are pressed against each other.

"Dalton!" She draws out the last syllable as tremors overtake her.

Her grip on my arm is a vise. I love every minute of it.

Her voice devolves into a long squeal, then a breathy exhale. With one more clench on my hand, she relaxes, her arms falling to the bed. Her back collapses into place. And I didn't even get her naked.

I continue to stroke her gently, taking my time learning these intimate parts of her. There's a softness to her inner thighs, then a firmness to her skin around her pelvic bones. She's not bare, a small thatch of hair at the crest of her labia.

I smile at my technical terms.

Nadia bumps my arm. "What's funny?"

"I might be examining you and using the correct anatomical language in my head."

She thumps me again. "Like what?"

"Labia majora." I rub my thumb along it, then slip closer to the center. "Labia minora."

She laughs and nudges me again. "Just call it my pussy."

I peer into the dark corner where I assume the cats are. "But we have so much of that."

This gets me a good whack on the shoulder.

I lean into her ear. "What do your books call it?"

I feel her smile against my cheek. "Hmm. Her sex. Her core. Her essence."

"That's all wrong. Sex should mean *female* in this case, core is abdominals, and essence, I don't know, your perfume."

This makes her laugh. "Better than calling it my hot pocket."

"Oooh, I like that."

"My hot pocket."

I grip it more tightly. "It's a hot little pocket."

"Are you going to put something in it?"

I suck in a breath. "Hell, yes, I am."

23

NADIA

I never talk dirty.

I'm not sure why I'm doing it. Maybe because the irresistible doctor who's been sleeping under the same roof as me is finally acting on all the things we've both been clearly thinking about.

Or possibly it's because he knows the books I read, something I've never let anyone see. And it's an undercurrent between us, those soft sex scenes, the act out in the open, nothing to hide, consensual, hot, and in great detail.

Dalton makes it feel like it's all coming to life.

He pushes my shirt up and over my head. Funny how I got all the way to orgasm without removing any clothes.

Then his mouth is on my belly, grasping the elastic of my shorts with his teeth. He tries to pull them off that way, but I have too much hip, and we both laugh as he wrestles them down.

His fingers slip beneath the lacy edge of my panties.

He's already been all these places, but as he eases them over my thighs, his breath caressing my skin, it's still so new.

I've been here with other men, but Dalton is so attentive, like I'm something precious to behold.

He kisses random places. My ankle. My knee. The jutting bone of my hip. Then he's back at my mouth. Somewhere along the way, he shed his own clothes. The feel of our full bodies against each other is so intimate, so beautiful, that for a second, tears sting my eyes.

How did we get to this place? I feel like I know him so well, what he wears, how he eats, his routines. But I've never known this, the warmth of his skin, the strength of his arms, the smoothness of his chest against mine.

I could live in this moment for the rest of my life, sated but curious, happy but wanting more, relaxed but also filled with anticipation.

He brushes his thumb across my cheek. "Condom okay?"

I nod. We can graduate to other methods later, after more discussion. He reaches over to his drawer in the nightstand. When a wrapper crinkles, I ask, "Have those been there all along?"

"Yes."

"Right beside us."

"Waiting." He shifts to his side.

I can barely make out his shadow, and the movement of the condom over him is impossible to see in the dark.

I reach out to run my hands over his chest, learning

every muscle and valley, the heat of his skin, and the trail of hair leading down to his—

What did they call it in the books?

Cock? Erection? Sword? I smile in the dark. *Pickle.*

I reach for it, feeling the bump of the lip of the condom and run my fingers lightly along the length. I should have done this before he put it on.

Another night.

And it hits me that I can do this whenever I like. There is no need for dates or restaurants or a dance of *will he or won't he call?*

He's right here. He lives here.

I grip him with some pressure, and he sucks in a breath. "Nadia…"

What do I want this first time? Something traditional, with him on top of me? Do I want to ride him in his lap? Him behind me? Side-by-side? On the edge of the bed?

So many possibilities.

But as he crawls over my body, kissing his way over my skin, I let him take the lead. With so much time ahead of us, we can explore. Every position. Every way to connect.

When his naked body is over mine, it feels completely right. Like he's come home. Like this was always meant to be. He brushes loose hair off my forehead, kissing along my jaw. His mouth claims mine again, and it's glorious to realize I already recognize the taste of him. Another part of Dalton I know.

"I can't believe we're here," he whispers against my hair.

"I know. I always thought we considered this part more the day we met than on any other day."

He chuckles. "Maybe you thought it more that day."

I smile against his forehead. "You're right. I definitely thought about it after seeing you naked coming out of the shower."

"I may have thought about it almost every day."

"Really?" He never showed it.

His fingers glide along the side of my breast and down my waist to slip inside me again.

My chin lifts, and I suck in a breath. I can't believe I want more. I felt so relaxed and sated a minute ago. But now I want him. I want all of him inside me.

"Dalton?"

He knows what I'm asking. Why I'm saying his name. He shifts again, sliding my thighs open with his knee. The sheets beneath my legs feel silky and cool. It's decidedly sexy, parting for him.

Then he's there, moving aside his hand to slip inside me.

I gasp as he moves, sending a cascade of pleasure up my body. I see sparks in the dark, maybe those hormones he once talked about. I clutch his back, my knees brushing his elbows as he holds himself over me.

Forget what I said before. This is the part I never want to end. It's so easy, so glorious, utterly perfect. Tears squeeze from my eyes. This is Dalton. Dalton and me. How we work together on the most intimate level.

His lips brush my forehead. I hadn't expected the tenderness, although I should have known. The cats. His mom. His job. He cares. A lot. He's not like the MMA fighters, and maybe even kinder than Max.

My chest expands and I wonder if there will be room here for actual love.

Then Dalton speeds up and all the soft thoughts are obliterated as my body responds. God, he's got me, and I'm utterly rapt at his every move.

The center of me quivers around him, and I know it's coming again. Again? Has it ever happened twice for me?

He moves his hand between us, fingers circling my most sensitive spot.

The intensity leaps to a new level. I squeeze my eyes shut, my chin in the air. My back arches as the orgasm takes over. I'm full of light, expanding, drawing in the universe.

I vaguely hear myself crying his name, lost in the pleasure overtaking every part of my body.

Dalton draws it out, plunging into me, working my clit, his mouth near my ear. He's saying my name, over and over. "Nadia, Nadia." There's a desperate note in it that clutches at my heart.

I hold him tightly, collapsing his arms to bring his chest to mine. We slow down as the stars fall around us, the room going quiet, breathing returning to its regular cadence.

He slips to the side and draws me to him, pulling my leg over his hips. We don't quite separate, not yet, and I feel him twitching inside me.

He presses my head to his chest. We lie there for

long moments, his heartbeat a gentle thud against my cheek.

This changes everything, I realize. Will I sleep beside him? No more air mattress? No distance?

Does everything shift from his and mine to *ours*? The storage, the space, the fridge?

I'm overthinking it. I clear my head so that I might relax in his arms.

He kisses my hair again, and it might be my favorite thing that he does. A warm glow rises in me. There is no need to think beyond this moment.

But then a quiet *mew* pierces the dark.

Then another.

We try to ignore it, but then it becomes a chorus.

Both of our bellies shake with the effort of not laughing.

"Is it your turn or mine?" I ask.

"I'll do it," he says.

"I'll help."

And so we slide apart, searching for our clothes. Dalton discards the condom in a Kleenex.

No matter what happens with the bed situation or how we view being roommates after this, the kitty parenting duties are definitely *ours*.

24

DALTON

I'm never sure exactly what tipped Nadia and me into this new relationship, but I don't question it.

The next two weeks are nothing short of perfect. The kittens get stronger. The mama cat takes over the feedings. They all learn how to use the litter box. And the end of every shift finds me home with Nadia, never too tired to strip her naked and have my way with her.

Our lives are a long string of cats, showers, meals, and sex.

I finally get my shot at assisting in an advanced procedure at the hospital, and I feel considerably more doctor-like.

Nadia comes up with the clever idea of a pickle breaded in crumbled spicy Cheetos, named the Hot Pickle, which becomes a colossal hit after making the rounds on social media.

We discover we both love 80s sitcoms and spend hours cuddled with the cats watching the *Golden Girls* and *Cheers*.

One night, as I'm running my tongue along the side of her waist, searching for any spot I haven't yet tasted, I look up to see her, watching me with those warm eyes and something expands in my chest.

Before my thinking brain can jump in and slow me down, I find myself saying, "I love you."

Her eyes widen.

My immediate reaction is to try to take it back. This was too fast. It's only been a few weeks since we first slept together, only a couple of months since we met.

As my brain frantically tries to come up with a way to play off the words, Nadia reaches out to press a warm hand on my shoulder. "I understand what you're saying. It's been tender between us for a long time. Since the cats, maybe?"

The adrenaline starts to drain. Maybe I didn't screw up.

"I think so."

"Have you been in love before?" she asks. "Or is it bad luck to talk about exes when we're naked?"

"Only if I'm inside you when I answer."

She laughs.

I sit against the wall, my legs straight out on the bed. I drag her body over to mine, arranging her knees on either side of my thighs.

Then I grasp her hips and yank her body toward mine, sliding inside her with a swift, powerful stroke.

She sucks in a breath. "Shit," she says, and I smile that I've brought her to cursing. It's rare.

"Still wanna know?" I ask.

"Maybe not yet." Her voice is jagged and raw.

I hold on to her hips, rocking her against me. I set the pace, but then she lifts her body up and slams it down on mine. I love it when she takes control.

She grabs both my wrists and pins them against the wall. Her breasts shift in front of me, tantalizing and soft. The sight of her naked and in charge makes me outrageously hot.

She moves faster and faster, and I close my eyes, feeling the hard slam of her body as it connects to mine, the friction as I move inside her. She presses hard on my wrists as she grinds down, rotating in tiny circles on my lap.

Damn. We're ridiculously compatible. We read each other's minds. Although sometimes, we can completely surprise each other.

Her voice rises in its keening cry. My name is mixed with other garbled words.

I love this. I feel it when her body clamps down on mine. The tightness threatens to set me off, but I hold back a little longer until that specific point in her cry that tells me she's hit her max.

She gets there, and my control is lost, my whole body suffused with the intensity of filling her.

Nadia collapses against my chest, and I hold her tightly now that my arms are on my own again. We breathe against each other for a moment, and then she says, "You're still inside me. Have you been in love before?" It's almost as if the conversation never paused.

It's an easy answer. I wrap an arm around her neck. "No. You are my first."

I decide not to ask her the same question. I don't

want to know the answer. It doesn't matter to me. I'm in the now, and this present moment is all about Nadia.

The cats have come to understand when we're available and when we're not. Since the room has quieted, the bed thumps with the arrival of six sets of paws, two grown and four tiny.

Catzilla lies against Nadia's leg. Mama Cat curls next to her. They are all properly aside, not completely invading our space.

The kittens, however, have no such social graces. They crawl over Nadia's thighs, falling into the space between us. A tiny claw pierces my belly.

"Hey!" I say, lifting the offender, Ferris Mewler, as usual. I bring his white face to mine. "Have a little delicacy!"

Nadia laughs hard enough that she pushes me right out of her. And that's it. Clean up must happen or we'll be washing cats.

She picks up the kittens and sets them aside. "Make your escape."

I do, heading for the bathroom. "Of course you can shower with me. The cats won't follow us there, water and all."

She considers it. "Okay. You've convinced me."

I hold out my hand and she takes it, and our life together continues its glorious rise and fall beneath the warm spray.

I've never known a time like this.

The intern games are the next day. In them, teams from surgery, maternity, oncology, and emergency compete in various hospital-themed challenges.

Maybe I got less sleep than I should have, up with Nadia half the night, but I feel invincible, like I am drunk on happiness and sleep is optional.

Harrington, Fitz, and I team up. We all convene in the last curtain row of the ER, the one least used, particularly on a weekday morning.

The nurses have moved the row aside to give us extra space.

The first challenge is the PPE race, where we have to locate and put on a mask, hairnet, gown, gloves, goggles, and shoe covering.

We need two members.

"I'm a total klutz," Harrington says. "Dalton, you and Fitz go."

"I concur," Fitz says. "Harrington would trip on a spider."

Oncology chooses two interns. I eyeball the PPE strewn about. Gloves should go last, since they will slow me down. Shoe covers next to last, as they can be slippery. Goggles also late, since it's harder to see. But masks make it harder to breathe.

Then it's too late to strategize. Booker lifts her arm and shouts, "Go!"

"We should collect first," Fitz hisses as we dive beneath a gurney to grab goggles.

Right. Collect and then put it on.

The other team hasn't thought of this, pausing to shove caps on their heads. They realize their mistake when one of them ducks beneath the gurney to get goggles and the hat gets caught on a knob. They lose precious time pulling it off.

Not all the items are grouped. There's only one gown in the stack, so I leave it to Fitz and search out the other items. I feel light, springing over a stool to snatch up a pair of shoe covers and leaping high into the air to snag a mask, which are dangling from where they are tucked into the noise dampening ceiling tiles.

Fitz is height challenged, so I leap a second time for hers and toss it her way. "Thanks!" she says.

Neither member of oncology can jump that high, so they are forced to drag a stool over.

My heart is pumping as I slide beneath a sink to snag a partially hidden gown. This challenge is an obstacle course, scavenger hunt, and dressing challenge all in one.

The caps are on the counter but where are the gloves? I open cabinets, finally finding a pair in a drawer. Almost there. I drop it all on an empty bed to start dressing.

Gown. Shoe covers. Mask. Cap. Goggles. The gloves are hard on my sweaty palms.

Fitz is still trying to find gloves. "Murphy!" she calls.

Right. I leave my goggles on my head and start searching.

Oncology has acquired everything and are dressing.

"You dress and I'll search," I tell Fitz.

She starts madly shoving her arms in the gown.

Where are those last gloves?

I spot a gurney in the corner with a suspicious lump

beneath the paper sheet. I press my hands into the bed between me and it, hopping over the mattress in a clean jump.

Yes, it's gloves.

Oncology is trying to get their gloves on. Fitz is tying her gown. She looks up.

"Catch!" I yell at her and fling the gloves across the room.

She snags them, and her cool confidence saves her as the gloves, which are probably a size too small for the rest of us, slide onto her hands easily.

We dash for Booker seconds before oncology gets their gloves on.

Booker nods and turns toward the lead resident for oncology. "Told you my interns were superior."

It's a small victory, but we'll take it.

When a nurse snaps our picture as the winners, I forward the image on to Nadia with the text "You make me invincible."

Because she does.

25

NADIA

"You're singing." Jeannie's words are an accusation. She punctuates it with a hard thwack of a knife, cleaving the end of an onion from the rest of its bulb.

"Sorry." I reduce to a low hum as I slice pickles in the deli kitchen.

"Is that an overwrought ditty from a sappy movie?"

The song is "Till There Was You" from *The Music Man*, but I don't think Jeannie is really asking for a title, so I simply say, "It is!" and keep slicing.

The kitchen door opens. I look up, expecting to see Vera or Geneva replenishing the line, but instead, it's Hex.

What does he want? I'm about to let him know I'm with someone when he shoves a fistful of flowers close to Jeannie's face. "I brought you these."

Jeannie takes a step back, wrinkling her nose. "If you get pollen on my onions, by God I will use your face to chop a new batch."

I bite my lip to keep from laughing. I had forgotten

that Hex had taken a shine to Jeannie when I turned him down after the hospital incident.

Hex is undeterred. "I will put them in Max's office." He hurries off.

"Where they will die a lonely death," she mutters.

I transfer my sliced dills to a bin. "Not much into romantic gestures?"

She aims the pointy end of her knife at me. "Entanglements are a distraction. I am a bastion of focus." She glances at my bin. "Double that."

"Aye, aye, captain," I tell her, pulling additional pickles from the bucket.

Hex returns. "With my gifts bestowed, I will take my leave." He bows deeply, bent over so that his head is even with the counter, which looks hilarious on his enormous frame in a T-shirt and gym shorts.

"Next time dress better," Jeannie says.

His face lights up. "I will." He seems chuffed that she has hinted that he should return as he passes back through the door.

"You practically proposed marriage, you know," I tell her. "He was only expecting to be thrown out."

She frowns. "I was trying to insult him."

"He caught you off guard." I want to laugh at this entire situation, but I know better. It's cute. I'm rooting for Hex.

I finish my pickles and carry the bins to the walk-in. I came in early, so I'm officially off duty.

When the gloves are in the trash and my apron is in the laundry pile, I collect my purse and head out the back door.

The sun is shining broadly, and I feel so happy I want to skip. Dalton won't be home, not until tomorrow morning, but there are kitties to play with, food to cook, and a day with him to look forward to.

Is this love? I wonder. My body is light, like I'm not quite walking on the ground.

Jeannie noticed. I have told no one about Dalton's move from roommate to lover. But maybe it's becoming obvious. And I almost told Hex right in front of her.

I should tell my family.

No, they might judge me. The roommate situation was bad enough.

I can imagine my dad giving me a speech. "Nadia, you're being irresponsible and flighty. You barely knew this boy when you moved in, and now you're in love? What has gotten into you?"

Mom would get it. She's a romantic.

Probably not Max, though. I better keep it to myself for a while longer. When a few months have passed, it might be all right to say we're dating. It will make more sense.

I open up my Jeep, patting the little rubber ducks Dalton has been leaving on my dash. I didn't even know Jeeps and ducks were a thing until he left the first one, tiny and bright and decorated with a smattering of red hearts.

That one has been joined by a duck holding a black kitty, and another reading a book.

Our life together, in ducks.

I play the soundtrack to *The Music Man* as I drive home. Dalton and I watched it a few nights ago. I don't think he's into musicals, but he is into me, and that's enough.

I feel so lucky. How did this happen? So what if I'm working in a deli? I'm paying the bills. The future can wait.

It occurs to me that I could end up a doctor's wife.
Whoa.
Slow down, girl. You're in the glory days. The easy part.

But as the colorful awnings of bright shops whiz by, anything seems possible.

When I pull up to the slot near our apartment, I peer through the windshield. Did some paint come off the front door? There's a strange triangle of white.

I jump out of the Jeep. Only when I get closer do I realize it's a piece of paper flapping in the breeze. A notice.

It could be anything. Painting the railing. Pest control. Upgrading an appliance. Routine maintenance.

But my belly quakes just the same.

I reach out and pull it down. The cats have heard my footsteps and meow for me to come in.

But I wait a moment so I can scan it.

Dear Residents of Apartment <u>1405</u>:

It has come to our attention that you have pets. Under the terms of your rental agreement, all pets must be approved by management and be accompanied by a deposit and a monthly rental fee.

Additionally, your pets violate the following terms:

. . .

I scan the list.

Over 50 pounds.

Banned Breeds.

There is a check mark halfway down.

Number of pets exceed the limit of two.

I glance up. How did they know?

Next to the door, the lone window to the outside winks at me. It's the white blinds, moving back and forth.

What in the world?

I step closer.

A white paw peeks between the slats, moving them aside. Then a face. Ferris Mewler.

"Ferris!"

Soon he's joined by a gray face. Greyson. Then a flash of orange. Pumpkin. Then a black set of ears. Doppelgänger.

So that's what happened. The kittens discovered the window. Someone walked by. Maintenance. One of the office workers. And they knew.

Since I can see where the kittens are, I quickly unlock the door and dart inside.

Mama Cat and Catzilla lie together on the sofa. The kittens turn to me, leaping from the sill to the arm of the sofa. They got big. They got brave.

They got busted.

I sit on the sofa to read the rest of the notice, quickly swarmed over by cats.

Pursuant to your rental agreement, you must immediately remove the pets from your premises or pay the deposit and fees, and comply with any additional violations.

Your apartment will be inspected on <u>September 16</u>. If you are in violation again, you will be evicted with no refund of your deposit.

That's in two days! I can't re-home the cats that quickly!

I glance over at Catzilla and MC. They are licking each other.

How could I separate them? Catzilla is so happy to have a bestie.

Hopelessness washes over me. What will I do?

I unlock my phone to text Dalton.

The cats have been discovered. I have two days to remove four.

Tears drip onto the smooth surface. What will we do?

I don't expect to hear from him right away. If he's seeing a patient, or under direct scrutiny by a supervisor, he won't risk even checking it.

The kittens circle my lap, meowing for attention, for treats, for food.

I carefully extricate them from my jeans and fill the line of bowls. The adult cats watch as the kittens guzzle their dinner. I always feed them separately as the hungry babies will steal their adult kibble otherwise.

When they are settled, I lean against the bar, looking over the room.

I don't know what's next for me. All I do know is that these cats are mine. My kittens. My family.

But we can't all live here.

26

DALTON

I read Nadia's texts around midnight with a feeling of doom.

So, it's happened.

Damn.

She sent an image of the notice on the door.

We're screwed. We only have two days.

She's probably asleep by now, but I write her back, anyway.

This sucks. We'll figure something out.

But will we?

Finding that place had been hard enough. How could we get another?

I will have to try.

Fitz bumps my shoulder as she sits beside me in the break room. "What's got you so long in the face?"

"Cat kids got busted. We have to find them a home or move out."

Harrington takes a chair opposite me. "Your girl won't let those cats go."

"I don't want them to go either. And where would we take them? The shelters are full. The rescues are full."

Fitz shakes her head. "People need to neuter their animals."

"They were strays."

"They came from somewhere." She shoves a fork into her plastic bowl filled with pasta.

I unwrap a sandwich. "You two wouldn't have spots, would you?"

"My roommates would murder me in my sleep," Fitz says, using her fork as a pretend knife slashing her throat. "Manny petted a neighbor's cat, and Veronica made him wash his hands for thirty minutes before he could touch her stuff. She has a thing about dander."

I nod. "Nadia's cousin is allergic."

"I can't keep a plant alive," Harrington says. "And I'm pretty sure my place doesn't allow pets at all."

I sit back in my chair. "We're up a creek."

Fitz stabs a noodle. "Sounds like it."

The night goes slowly. Monday nights often do. I see a UTI, two chest pain cases, and a dehydrated pregnant woman.

When I get off around seven, for the first time in a long time, I dread going home.

I pull in next to Nadia's blue jeep. I open my glove compartment. I got another duck for her, this time a pink one. I'm not sure it will make a dent in cheering her up.

When I've set it on her door handle so she'll be sure

to notice it, per the rules of DuckDuckJeep, I steel myself and head to our apartment.

Our apartment. Those words have taken on a new meaning since we've been together as a couple rather than roommates. I assume we'll move together, even though in any other circumstance it would be madness to cohabitate after only a few weeks of getting romantically involved.

Is it madness? Should we separate and date normally?

Who would get the cats?

Her, obviously. My shifts are too long.

I open the front door carefully to make sure no cats escape.

Nadia is up, sitting cross-legged on the floor for the kittens to climb like a jungle gym.

"Hey," I say, setting my phone and keys on the bar. "How are you holding up?"

Her face crumples, and I can see by the red rims of her eyes that she's been crying.

I sit next to her. Ferris Mewler immediately leaps from her to me in a flash of white. "That bad, huh?"

She leans over, resting her head on my shoulder. "What are we going to do?"

"I have twenty-four off. Let's look for a new place." I guess that decision was already made in my head, madness or not.

Her head pops up. "You think so?"

"Maybe we have to look farther afield. Maybe we'll get lucky."

She moves the other three kittens to my lap and

hops to her feet. "I'll get a notepad. We can figure out a budget, then start looking. Maybe there's something off the beaten path. Maybe someone has a garage apartment, or a tiny home. You know, not part of a corporate complex with strict rules."

"Sounds like a plan."

She sits at the bar, an open notepad in front of her. "We could easily afford this place together. Do you think we could go up four hundred?"

"I think so." Although that's less to send to my mother. She'd been able to quit her previous crappy job and spend a couple of weeks looking for the next one with my help. Hopefully, she'll last at this new one for more than a few months.

"Of course, the cats are an expense. They will all need shots soon. And vet appointments aren't cheap. I wonder if it's one fee for all of them. Surely it is. I don't think they charged me extra when I brought them all in."

I hadn't thought about all that. I remember what Fitz said. "They'll all need neutering soon."

Nadia frowns. "Oh, that's going to be expensive. I'll call around and see who might give us a deal on all four."

I pick Greyson off my shoulder where his claws are digging in. "Mama needs neutering too. She's probably getting well enough."

"Five surgeries," Nadia mutters, scribbling numbers on the pad. "Maybe I can plead with one of the rescues to help with the cost. They usually get lower rates with veterinarians who work with them."

Pumpkin leaps onto Greyson's back, making him hiss. I let them tussle. Kittens learn a lot through play.

Nadia holds her head in her hands. "I'm going to have to get a proper job to support the cats." She drops the pen. "I don't want to run any more numbers."

She leaves the stool to sit down beside us like before. "I wish I could play with them and pretend we don't have any worries."

I spot the notice folded up near the sofa and lean over to pick it up. "Do you think they'll kick us out on the 16th or that's just when they tell us?"

"I don't know." Her voice is tear-filled. "They'll have to let us pack."

"We're going to lose the deposit."

"I'll scrape up another one."

I'll have to scrape, too. I lie back on the carpet and stare at the ceiling. I don't begrudge Nadia for saving the kittens, not in the least. But they sure have made our situation much more complicated.

27

NADIA

Dalton and I call everywhere for two days, looking for a new place. Everything is too expensive, or they won't let us keep the cats.

I consider trying to part with them and call the rescues again. I even offer to volunteer in their offices, do administrative work to help pay for them.

One of them is willing to take only the kittens, and another only the Mama Cat, but I can't bear to separate them, so I do nothing.

I'm alone in the apartment on the 16th when I get a hard knock on the door.

I peer out the blinds. It's Evan from the office, plus a man from maintenance.

They're here.

What if I pretend I'm not?

I text Dalton as I sit quietly on the sofa, pausing only to occasionally snatch a kitten before it can mess with the blinds and show itself.

Me: Evan and a maintenance guy are here. What do I do?

I don't expect an answer, but as the time lengthens and there's another knock, louder this time, I panic a little more.

Me: I know you won't get a message while you're with patients and I don't expect an answer. I'm nervous. They have keys to get in here. That's probably why Evan brought maintenance.

Miraculously, I get a message back.

Dalton: Grab the cats and go in the bathroom. Turn on the shower. They'll back out even if they come in.

That's a good idea. I snatch up the open crate and dump all the kittens and a surprised Mama Cat into it. Catzilla is startled by my sudden movements and dashes under the bed.

Close enough.

I race into the bathroom and set the box down, lunging for the faucets.

I've barely got the spray going when the kittens leap out and start sniffing around.

I lock the door and sit by it, listening, petting the cats so they won't make noise.

Maybe the front door opens. Maybe it doesn't. The spray is loud.

It's possible I hear voices. But maybe not.

I wait until it gets steamy and uncomfortable in the bathroom, then I twist off faucets. I'm wasting water.

And I wait some more.

Dalton: Hiding in the supply closet to check on you. What's happening?

Me: Also hiding. Still in the bathroom.

Dalton: Keep me updated.

I sit there, my panicked brain searching for a solution to our dilemma.

Pitch a tent in Max's back yard. Get an Air B&B for a few days. A cheap one, if I can find one.

But those things aren't permanent solutions.

The fact is, I either have to give up the cats or give up living in LA.

Then the answer comes to me.

I don't like it.

Dalton won't like it, either

But it's what has to happen if I want to keep the cats.

I have to go home.

If I do that, Dalton could keep the apartment. Evan could come in to inspect the place whenever he wanted. The cats and I could be gone.

I think and think, but the more I consider it, the more I know this is the solution. My parents love animals, but are currently petless. They have a big house.

When the kittens are bigger, maybe I can give one to my brother Axel, who lives on the other side of the woods from my parents. My brother Court might take a couple of them. They love having barn cats.

My throat grows thick. I pick up Greyson, Pumpkin, Doppelgänger, and Ferris Mewler. Can I let them go? Tears drip from my eyes.

There's another risk. If I go home, how long until my family makes me go to work for Pickle Media?

And what about Dalton? I'd be leaving him, living

two states away in Colorado. We're so new. Would he wait for me to come back? Is that too much to ask?

I lie on the rug, the kittens crawling over me.

I'm afraid to leave the room. It's cozy in here with all the cats. If I go out there, I have to face my decision. Start packing.

Leave Dalton.

I lie back down and Mama Cat walks up to sit close to my head, kneading her paws gently in my hair.

"Thanks for the biscuits," I tell her, but my voice cracks.

The kittens settle all over me, my belly, on my legs. Ferris curls into my neck.

There's no hope that they were merely trying to scare us with the notice. They came today, and they'll come again in a few hours, or tonight, or tomorrow.

I wipe the tears from my eyes. Might as well put the plan into action.

I text Max first.

Me: Got busted with the cats. Going to drive home with them tonight. I'll come back to help at the deli when you need me, especially when the baby comes.

Max: What? Tonight?

Me: Have to. They already came over to evict us. Going to let my roommate keep the place since he works at the hospital.

I swallow hard at the word *roommate*. Like Dalton was never anything more. But we never announced it. We didn't think about it. In our quiet space, it didn't seem necessary.

Max: You sure there's no place to go? I could ask around.

Me: For me and six cats? That's a lot for anybody.

Max: You want me to help you load up?

Me: There's not much. Dalton will help.

Max: Cam and I are due for a visit to the homestead. We'll make it sooner rather than later to see how you're doing.

Me: That will be nice.

Max: Chin up. My dad will come for you now, you know. He's really pushing for you to go to Florida with your brother.

Me: I know. Don't tell him yet, okay? I bought myself some time.

Max: You can count on me.

I try to think of what to text Dalton, but nothing comes. He'll be off this evening. I'm not sure I can avoid Evan or maintenance a second time. How many showers in one day will they believe?

Actually, I'll explain the situation. Meet with Evan, tell them Dalton and I broke up over the problem, and I'm moving out, but Dalton will stay. If there are any fees, I'll pay them.

Then I can wait for him to come.

And then I'll go.

It's going to suck. And I'm already crying again just thinking about it.

But it's the only way.

28

DALTON

I try a hundred ways to get off shift early, but Booker is on a rampage about Fitz being late and takes it out on us all. I don't cut loose of the hospital until well after eleven that night.

Nadia has been oddly silent other than to confirm that nobody has knocked on our door again.

She doesn't think they entered the apartment because when she left the bathroom, Catzilla was sleeping on the sofa. If strangers had invaded for even a minute, she wouldn't have come out for hours.

The lights are all on, though. She's stayed up waiting for me. I'm not the least bit fatigued due to the anxiety over our predicament, so I'm ready for us to stay up and figure out our next move.

I unlock the door and open it slowly to watch for errant kittens.

Ferris pokes his white head in the crack but he appears to be acting alone. I scoop him up and slip inside.

"He got away from me," Nadia says. She sits cross-legged in the middle of the room, surrounded with cats. They are wired, jumping over her legs into the valley in the middle, then leaping out to circle around her back.

I drop my pack on the sofa and settle next to her. Ferris crawls along my leg, clawing my scrubs. I've been finding tiny holes in all my workwear. "Come here, you little beast," I tell him and lift him away to curl into my hand. He'll be too big for this trick soon.

Something about the room feels off. I glance around and realize all of Nadia's luggage is lined up in the space between the bed and the dresser.

"Did you find a new place?" I ask. Happy anticipation of her answer makes my chest expand.

But her hesitation flips the switch. My chest tightens, and my throat constricts. I let out a slow breath. "What is it?"

She won't meet my gaze, keeping her eye on Pumpkin, who has plopped down in her lap. "I'm going home. All the way home. To my parents."

Shock thunders through me. "In Boulder?"

"Yes. I already went to the office to talk with Evan. I told him we had a big argument about the cats and broke up. I turned in my key and said you would be staying, no pets. He didn't charge me any fines or anything, which was nice, because he could have."

It takes a few seconds for everything she's said to sink in. "You turned in your key? You're giving up?"

"If you have trouble with rent on your own, I can probably help, especially when I start working. I know you said when we got this place that it was more than you wanted to pay."

"No, I won't let you do that." My stomach feels like it's lined with concrete. Vagus nerve stimulated. That mind-body connection is fierce. The unease gets worse as I ask, "Did you already take a job with your family?"

"No. Max has promised not to tell Uncle Sherman that I've left LA."

"Your cousin knew before me?" My whole body buzzes. *Calm down*, I tell my brain. *Enough with the cortisol.*

"You were busy. I didn't want to upset you at work." She shifts closer to me, resting her head on my shoulder. "I couldn't think of any other way."

"What happens to us, then?"

"I don't know anything yet, Dalton. I'm going to let the kittens get bigger, then maybe my brothers will take one or two, and maybe some will stay with my parents. If I can bear to split them up."

"Then you'll come back?" I wrap an arm around her waist.

"Maybe? I have some reckoning to do with my family."

So she might not.

The word love hasn't come up much since I said it the first time. I have occasionally whispered it to her again in the dark.

But I don't think she feels it. That's why this is easier for her.

It makes sense. It was fast. We dove into this like teenagers.

Or I did.

Mama Cat leaps off the sofa to move to the cat bed, drawing the kittens. They abandon us to see if she will let them have milk. She's been trying to wean them. They're old enough.

I pull Nadia to my lap. "I'm not going to let you go."

She turns to straddle me, smoothing my hair off my forehead. "It's not a breakup. I'll do whatever I can to get back here."

That's something, at least. "I'm stuck in LA. I can't transfer to a new hospital mid-internship."

"I wouldn't let you do that, anyway. This is so new for making life changes."

She means us. I get that. It's just that I feel like I've loved her all my life.

"Hey," she says. "We'll be all right. Would it help if we planned a little? When can you transfer?"

"After a year. So next summer." It's only fall.

"That's not long." She kisses my forehead.

"Without you? That's an eternity." I hold her more tightly.

"We'll make it." Her words are warm against my ear.

I take in everything about her like it's the last time. The smell of floral shampoo in her hair. The fit of her head against my neck. I run my hands from her waist to her hips, committing the feel of her to memory.

She presses her mouth to my cheek, and I turn, settling my lips on hers. The kiss deepens quickly, and soon we're undressing, shirts falling to the carpet in a whisper, skin to skin.

She's warm and soft and I want to memorize everything about her, to make sure there's nothing I missed. The crook of her elbow, the back of her knee, the wisps of hair over her ear.

I've never used the phrase *make love* before. It seems like something out of my grandparents' era. But those words rise up as I pull her panties down. I want to infuse her with everything I'm feeling, make an impression on every part of her body.

We're told as doctors that every system has a role. Endocrine. Respiratory. Digestion. Vascular. But the more I see people, the more I help them move from illness to recovery, the surer I am that every cell is imprinted with each experience. We're not made of parts. We are the whole of them together.

When I kiss her belly button, she sucks in a breath. And when I slide a finger inside her, her hips move with me, her memory aligning this experience with the ones from our history, a miracle of nerve endings and conscious thought and automatic response.

Past. Present. Will there be a future?

I kneel over her, using my free hand to touch everything, ribs, breasts, neck, shoulders. I cup her chin and kiss her again, wanting to sear her senses, to create something every part of her body remembers and misses, and hopefully, drives her to come back to me.

She gasps, already shifting upward toward climax. I slide over her and slip inside, touching her all the while. Her hands clasp my back, and each of my cells is infused with her.

A tear glimmers on her cheek, and I know emotion has overtaken her, a mix of signals. Exultation and despair. Connection and the preparation for loss. She feels something for me. Her body shows the signs.

Even with the sadness, she still tightens around me. I ignore the stinging in my own eyes and move with her, more deeply and in sync with her movements.

We arrive at the pinnacle together, her words crying out in the room we will soon no longer share. I wish this moment would never end, that we could remain clutched together until the planet ceased.

But then she starts weeping, and I draw her close. Her upset gives me hope that our bond will be strong enough to weather this.

We lie side by side, arms so tight that we are bundled as one, until at last she pulls away. "I'll sleep here tonight and leave in the morning. It doesn't make sense to go now."

I nod. We check on the cats, all snug with their mother, and go through our night routine that has become so familiar.

Then we curl together beneath her blue ruffles and my Optimus Prime, and sleep our last night in the same bed.

29

NADIA

I decide not to warn my parents ahead of time that I'm coming home, or that I have cats.

It's a grueling fourteen-hour drive. As the desert gives way to mountains, I realize that nobody knows anything about my life other than Dalton. Max knows about the cats, of course, but I haven't told anyone that Dalton is more than a roommate.

Or how hard it was to leave.

Now I have no one to talk about it with.

I go in and out of crying as the hours tick by. The cats are hard, yowling and miserable. It's difficult to get them to eat, or to use the litter box. Even though Catzilla has a big dog crate because of her size, it's still not a great situation for the six of them inside it for hours.

By the time I pull up to my parent's house late in the evening, I'm exhausted. But I can't simply turn the cats loose. The two-story stone house is huge, with an enormous open bottom floor plus an upstairs of bedrooms. I have to figure out where to contain them, or four errant kittens will easily get lost.

I'm relieved nobody's home, my mother's Infinity gone from the garage. It's a Friday night, so hopefully they are engaged in hours of something. Once the kitties are settled, I'll text them about my return and the cats so they know not to accidentally set them loose.

My old bedroom has its own bath, a privilege of being the only girl with three brothers. My parents built this house when I was in high school, and only Axel and I officially lived here. The boys shared a bathroom in the hall when they stayed during summers off and, later, holidays.

This will be a good space, but I'll have to kitten-proof everything.

I flip on the light. The cats are yowling but I don't dare let them out until I have set up a litter box and food dishes.

"Hold on, hold on." I set the crate on the floor by my bed. It's all still very high school here, boy band posters on the walls, and oh, the Biebs is up there.

I quickly collect all my blown-glass figurines from my dresser and hide them in a drawer. Those wouldn't last a hot second with the cats.

"One second, babies!" I say to them and race downstairs to my car. I snatch up the litter box and the paper bag with the kitty food and dishes.

I'm considerably slower heading back up. This is nuts. I'm dead on my feet from driving all day, cried out, and emotionally drained over leaving Dalton behind.

Over and over again, our last moments play in my

mind, the painful goodbye at dawn, Dalton barefoot in his T-shirt and running shorts. He refrained from telling me he loved me again, as if wringing the words out of me might hurt even more.

No, don't think about it now. Focus. Keep busy.

I set up the litter box under the vanity in my bathroom and make a line of cat dishes. I fill each bowl and add fresh water to two others.

"It's time!" I kneel to unlatch the crate.

An explosion of fur shoots out the door.

I sit back, watching to see what they will do.

Catzilla, remembering the room from previous visits, heads straight for the bathroom.

Mama Cat, realizing Catzilla is on to something, follows her.

But the kittens immediately start scaling the bed skirt. Ferris Mewler takes the lead, and Greyson isn't far behind.

Doppelgänger is the smallest of the bunch and gets stuck immediately. Pumpkin takes it slow and steady, but makes it up.

I tug Doppy off the fabric and set him on top with his siblings. They stand on the edge and mewl pitifully, as if I stranded them up there.

"Okay, okay." I gather the whole lot of them in my arms and walk them to the bathroom.

They spot Catzilla and Mama Cat eating and nearly squirm out. I kneel to let them zoom to the wet food I've left.

Whew.

All my suitcases are in the car, but I'm way too exhausted to think about hauling them up. Tomorrow.

I sit on the floor at the end of the bed. From here, I can see in the bathroom while I send all the necessary texts.

To Dalton: Made it home. Miss you already.

He's not at work yet, so he writes back quickly.

Dalton: The apartment is impossibly empty.

My throat tightens. It probably is harder for him. He's sitting in the midst of everything we had been.

Me: I'll do everything I can to get back to LA.

Dalton: I'll be here.

I lean back against the end of the bed and close my eyes. Tears threaten, but I refuse to give in. I'll figure this out. This is temporary.

Getting a job back in LA at a real salary is imperative. Finding something different to rent will be easier if I can afford more, maybe a house, or an independently owned condo with more lenient rules about pets.

The kittens stumble about, overfilled, tired. We're all road weary. Pumpkin approaches and crawls up on my lap, then falls asleep instantly.

I should go back to the car for the cat bed, but the whole crew makes their way up onto mine. I lift Doppelgänger so he won't have to fight it again, then carefully move Pumpkin to be with the others.

Probably there's room for me up there, but I'm not ready to fight it. I drag a clump of abandoned stuffed animals close to me and use them as a pillow.

Right as I'm about to wink out, I remember I was supposed to text my parents, too.

But I'm tired. I'll do it in a minute…

"Nadia?"

My head feels clogged, like I drank too much, like the morning after the hospital.

"Nadia? Are you okay?"

I open my bleary eyes. The sun is up. I slept all night.

Mom is looking down at me, a coffee cup in her hand. "I'm sorry to wake you, but I got worried. You came home without calling?"

I slowly pick myself up from the floor, stuffed animals scattered all around.

"Why are you sleeping down here?"

That's when I notice the open bedroom door.

Now I'm awake. I leap to my feet. "The kittens!" I race across the room and slam it closed. "Where are they?"

"Your big cat is right there," Mom says, pointing to Cattarina.

Cattarina sits on my pillows, but there are no other cats.

"The kittens! There are four! Plus their mother!" I frantically lunge for the bathroom. Mama Cat is there, licking the empty bowl. She looks at me accusingly, like I forgot to feed her this morning.

I peek in the litter box. No kittens. The shower curtain zips open with a jerk of my hand. Nothing.

Oh no, oh no, oh no.

I re-enter the bedroom. "Did you see them sneak by you when you came in?"

"I don't think so. You brought kittens with you?"

"Yes, that's why I'm here. I got kicked out of my apartment after I rescued them."

"You had an apartment? I thought you were staying with Max."

Uncle Sherman obviously hadn't squealed. I kneel to look under the bed. "Yes, for a while. Then I found these kittens. But the complex wouldn't allow me six cats."

"You signed a lease?" She's still confused, but I don't have time to tell her anything.

"I think they escaped. This house is too big!" I check beneath the dresser and under the edges of the curtains. The closet has been closed the whole time, but I open it anyway.

Mama Cat comes out to yowl at me for her breakfast. I snatch up the bag of dry and pour wildly into several bowls in the bathroom, then resume my search.

"What do they look like?"

"They're all different. One is white. Another mostly black. Pumpkin is orange. The fourth is gray."

"Let's go look then." She opens the door.

I follow her out, closing it behind me in case they are still inside somewhere.

In the hall, all the doors are open. Court's room. Rhett's. Axel's. The bathroom. Then there are the stairs.

"I'll take the upstairs, you go down," I tell Mom.

"Okay, Nadia. Don't worry. We'll find them. I'll tell

your father not to go outside until we've located them all."

"Thanks." I race into Axel's room, next to mine. It's plain, as he was almost graduated by the time we moved here, all navy blue and forest green. Only some track trophies and a few nature posters show his personality at all.

I zip through the room, peer under the bed, and listen for any sounds. Nothing.

The bathroom is easy to check. Empty.

Court's room is even plainer than Axel's, practically a guest room. He only ever stayed here during college breaks. It's gray and blue and empty of cats.

Rhett's room fits him, all black and maroon, moody and stark.

Still no cats.

I'm feeling panicked. Did they go downstairs? Did they tumble?

I call their names as I head downstairs. "Pumpkin? Doppelgänger? Greyson?" I make it down. "Ferris? Ferris?"

My mom spots me. "As in Bueller?"

"Mewler, actually."

Dad calls from the living room. "I think I might have what you're looking for."

I hurry past the front door and into the large room backed by floor to ceiling windows looking out on the mountainside.

Dad lies on the sofa, only his head visible from the back.

I hurry to him. Four kittens crawl all over him like he's a play scape at a park.

He lifts Ferris. "This one bites."

Relief flows over me. "They all do. They're learning."

I sit on the coffee table next to him. "Mom came in to check on me. I guess they snuck out."

Mom leans over the back of the sofa. "They're so little."

"Eight or nine weeks. I've had them a month."

"This is a lot of cats," Dad says.

Mom reaches out to pet Pumpkin. "They got her kicked out of the apartment we didn't know she had."

Dad peers up at me. "You moved out from Max's?"

"Cattarina was making Camryn sick. She's allergic."

"Oh," Mom says. "That makes sense. You should have told us. We could have helped."

"I was making money at Max's."

Dad lets out a scoffing laugh. "And you could afford a place in LA?"

"I had a roommate." I swallow hard. Nobody knows anything different about who Dalton was to me. *Is* to me.

"A roommate!" Mom sits at the end of the sofa, making Dad shift his feet. "Someone at the deli?"

"No, a doctor at the nearby hospital. He's an intern."

Dad's head snaps up at that. "He?"

Damn. Now I've done it.

"Don't be weird, Dad. It was just an arrangement." But my voice wavers at the end. They'll hear that.

And they do. They share a glance.

Mom picks up Greyson and sets him on her lap. "So you got kicked out over the cats. What about your roommate?"

"He kept the place."

"I see." She pets Greyson's soft head, and for her trouble, he rolls to his back and attacks her fingers.

"I need to let the kittens grow, get them fixed, and, I don't know, figure out what to do. No regular apartments are going to let me keep them all."

Dad lifts his three kittens all together in his big hands. "They're trouble. You going to adopt them out?"

"I don't know. I need a minute to figure out my next move."

My parents share another glance. "Sherman will want to be involved in that," Dad says. "He considers you a Pickle."

All three of us say, "Every Pickle's a Pickle," then laugh, startling the kittens. But I sober quickly. Uncle Sherman's insistence that I work for him is what's gotten me here.

Dad passes me Ferris. "Let's get these wildlings back in your room before they get lost. We can figure out a plan over breakfast."

I hold on to the white kitten, glad for a sounding board. For help.

It's good to be home.

But I wish Dalton were here.

DALTON

Going home feels pointless without Nadia there, so I spend less and less time at the apartment. I drive out to Harrington's place to eat pizza and drink beer. I meet Fitz and her boyfriend for burgers.

I shower and sleep in a place that used to feel like home.

About a week after Nadia left, Mom calls on one of my off days. She doesn't bother with pleasantries.

"Well, your old lady got fired again."

I sink onto the sofa. "What happened this time?"

"I told you about old Joe, the shift manager?"

"Right, the one who said you shouldn't fake being a redhead?"

Mom changes her hair color every season with drugstore dyes.

"Yeah, that one. He slapped my ass, and I punched his lights out. He went down like roadkill."

"And they fired you?"

"Nah, they fired both of us. If they'd just fired me, I'd have sued the pants off them."

I lean my head against the back of the sofa. "Are you going to be able to pay rent?"

"They won't do nothing over one month. You have to rack up three or four missed checks before they get testy."

"Mom, you shouldn't do that. You'll lose your deposit."

"This place sucks anyway."

I blow out a long breath, quietly, so it won't register on the call. "I'll call them and make the payment." Somehow.

"You can't do that, Baby D."

"Don't worry about it, Mom." That's my job. No more pizza or burgers for me. Or morning coffee at the hospital cart. I'll be eating ramen and brewing my own.

Maybe I can do DoorDash gigs during my twenty-four-hour breaks. Maybe I can get my med school loans reconfigured with lower payments. My brain buzzes with how I can help.

Mom's voice has an edge to it. "I'll get something soon. Everybody needs people. That's why you see old farts like me sacking groceries."

"Are you going to go apply for something?"

"Yeah, tomorrow. Or the next day. Soon. I'm being a lady of leisure at the moment. You doing all right? They treating you okay?"

"It's good."

"You send me pictures of your apartment, okay? I want to make sure my boy is someplace good."

"I will, Mom."

When she ends the call, I stare at the ceiling. I'll need an extra thousand to cover her rent.

It feels impossible. My blood pressure is rising, my heart rate increasing. I need to think of something else for a minute.

I close my eyes and picture Nadia, her skin, her eyelashes on her cheeks when she slept.

My phone is still on my thigh. I pick it up to text her.

Me: Got a minute?

We've texted constantly and talk long hours when we can. The kittens are exploring her parents' house. She's escaped notice from her uncle so far.

She's also started applying for jobs in LA, sending her resume far and wide. So far, no one's called her for an interview. But she's hopeful.

My phone buzzes with a call. I'm so relieved to see an image of her pop onto my screen. The contact picture is one I took of her sitting on the sofa with all the cats around her. It always makes me smile.

"Hey," I say.

"Hey." Her voice is like a balm to my frazzled brain. "Everything okay?"

Nothing is okay, I think. "Mom got fired again."

"Again?"

"You try to raise them right…"

She laughs. "I hope to meet her someday. Will you go there for the holidays?"

Now that's a question. I'm not sure how to squeeze in a flight across the country on my schedule. Or how to pay for it.

"I'll try. I don't know how many days I'll get. We'll likely be expected to work Christmas Eve."

"Will next year be better?"

"A little. Residents don't work the same crazy hours as interns."

"That will be a relief."

I'm so damn glad to talk to her. I want to reach through the phone and draw her close. But all I say is, "How are the kittens?"

"Ferris has figured out how to climb my curtains. They have a million little holes that make it look like stars when the sun shines through."

"See, he's an interior decorator."

She laughs. "The others are asleep on my bed."

"Did you ever find room for yourself?"

"We're figuring out bed boundaries."

I remember lying on the bed, the two of us both halves of a circle, the cats in the center. "I miss you."

Her voice catches. "I miss you, too. I'm a wreck. I don't think I've changed clothes in two days."

"That's all right. You're a single mom."

"I will pull myself together. I'm giving myself some grace."

I lie back on the sofa. "It's so quiet without you."

"I bet. I had a dream about you last night."

That gets my attention. "Did you?"

"It was very sexy."

"I've had those dreams, too."

"This is hard, isn't it?" Her voice has a note of despair in it.

"It's not forever."

She goes quiet. I wonder if she's giving up hope already.

"I love you, remember," I tell her. "I can wait however long it takes."

"I know. I do."

We're both quiet then, but the silence is all right. We're still connected, still in the same moment.

After a while, she says, "I'll talk to you soon, okay?"

"Okay, Nadia."

I set the phone on my belly. She's there, and I'm here. The distance feels impossible.

The apartment no longer smells of her. It didn't take long.

I force myself to get up and head to the kitchen. There's a leftover casserole she made in the fridge. I've been reluctant to eat it, not wanting the last piece of her to be gone.

But I take it out. It'll go bad otherwise.

She left all the dishes and pans for me, so this room feels like it always did. I lean against the counter, waiting on the microwave to ding.

I never realized that I was actually *living* until I stopped. Now it's all a grind again. Work, eat, sleep, try to keep my mother housed and fed.

I want my life back. I want Nadia back.

I need a home, not four walls.

Dinners, not reheated food.

Conversations, not mindless chatter.

The microwave finishes its cycle. I don't want to resent those kittens. I should aim my anger at the apartment complex for forcing our hand. Why should they refuse a litter if they were going to charge us extra and keep our deposit if the place got damaged?

And there's the matter of the lease. We could have gotten out of it if they kicked us out. But now I'm stuck here.

I stab the chicken and noodles, not wanting to eat. But I have another long shift coming up, and I need the fuel to get through it.

The savory bite nearly unravels me. It's like Nadia is here, sitting next to me, spooning it onto my plate. A meal. Nourishment. Company.

Real life.

I had it for a while.

And I don't know exactly how to get it back.

31
————
NADIA

This is torture.

I lie on my bed, letting the kittens crawl all over me.

The cats aren't torture. I fall more in love with them every day.

But being here. In my childhood bed. No job. No friends. Nothing to do but watch fur grow.

I shift to my side. "This was a bad idea," I tell Ferris, who bops me on the nose for my negativity. His tiny claws scrape my skin. I tap his head. "Be nice."

Mama Cat hears my tone and leaps onto the bed. She picks Ferris up by his scruffy white neck and jumps back down. Now that the kittens are getting more adventurous, she's been aggressive at keeping them in line.

"Thanks, MC," I tell her.

She plops Ferris next to Cattarina, who puts a meaty paw on the kitten's back, as if to say, "Don't do that again."

There's a knock at the door, louder and faster than Mom or Dad. My heart leaps for a moment, imagining Dalton is here, but that's dashed when my brother Axel's voice comes through. "Hey sis, you okay?"

"Yeah, watch for cats on the way in." I sometimes let the kittens have the run of the house, but this morning I didn't feel like chasing them down.

Axel opens the door, his shock of sandy brown hair appearing first. He watches the floor as he enters. "Got an attempted jailbreak," he says, scooping up the black body of Doppelgänger.

"Normally it's Ferris who makes the escape," I say. "But he's in time out." I wave over to the cat bed in the corner, where Cattarina holds vigil over Mr. Mewler, who is a fuzzy white blob at her massive feet.

He takes in the room. "Mom said you had six cats." He sits on the edge of the bed. He looks the same as always, mop of hair, scruffy beard, hiking boots and workout clothes. He's always tan from his daily mountain treks. He's known far and wide for hiking naked, although he bought an entire mountainside of property to make sure nobody encounters him.

You'd never know from looking at him that he has a net worth of half a billion from selling a hiking app before he even graduated college.

He might be my favorite brother, but don't tell Rhett and Court. They're salty enough as it is.

"You here to see Mom or what?" I ask. Axel and I have texted back and forth a few times since I returned, but he didn't say he was coming over today.

"Nah, they're not even home." Doppelgänger creeps

over the bed as if he's stalking Axel and is ready to pounce. Axel notices him. "You're fierce."

Doppy lets loose with a spring into the air, attaching himself to Axel's back.

I lean over and pull him off. "DopBeBop, we need to get you some toys."

"I can take you shopping, since you're unemployed."

"Send me a personal pet shopper. You can afford it."

He runs the back of his hands along his jaw. "I can. But the fun is in the discovery."

I swing my legs off the bed. "All right. Let's go."

He takes me in. "The sister I remember would never be caught dead in downtown Boulder in gray sweats and a messy bun. I like this new you."

My hands fly to my hair. I haven't gotten properly dressed or done any hair or makeup since I arrived. "I'm living up to my underachievement."

Axel's face twists into a frown. "You're the smartest of the bunch. Did this move from LA do a number on you? I heard you had a roommate. A boy roommate." He lightly punches my arm.

Doppy drops into another crouch, ready to pounce on Axel again.

"You get him, Dop," I tell the kitten. "Use all your black cat magic because he's asking questions that are none of his business."

Doppelgänger tightens his stance, shifting his little paws.

But Greyson has been watching from the pillow, and right when Dop is about to spring, Greyson leaps on top of him and bites his neck. They tumble in a blur of fur.

Axel laughs. "Saved by the sibling. Hey, there's four of them. You should have named them after us."

"Even the genders are right," I say. "Three boys and a girl."

He picks up Dop. "This one would be Rhett. Black like his soul."

"I think that would be our cousin Diesel."

It seems our cat toy excursion is delayed, so I sit back down. "I should call Diesel. Get some advice on avoiding Uncle Sherman."

"If you could find him. I don't think he's talked to anyone but Grammy Alma in a year."

"He didn't get sucked into Pickle Media."

"Neither did I."

"You got richer than Uncle Sherman."

Axel sighs, as if the money is a burden. "Maybe. It did get me out. I can get you out. I could make you my personal assistant."

I roll my eyes. "For what work? Scheduling your hikes? Definitely not for buying your wardrobe when you do them."

He grins. "Fair enough. I get it. So what do you want to do?"

"Get a job in LA. Find a place for my cats."

"Well, let's do it then."

"I've been applying. I haven't heard a single thing back from anyone. I don't have any experience."

"Let's get you some."

Dop and Greyson have stopped fighting and try to climb up Axel's back. He reaches around with more flexibility than I have and plucks them off to move them to his lap. "What would be the perfect job if you knew you could make enough money?"

That's easy. "I'd run a cat rescue."

"Okay, done. We'll start one. I'll bankroll it."

"Axel! You can't do that. Besides, I don't know anything about running a rescue. I need connections. Veterinarians. Volunteers. Paperwork. Permits."

"Then go work for one. Learn the ropes."

"I feel like a rescue is no way to make a living. They are always under-funded shoestring operations."

He nods. "I'd say let's cross that bridge when we come to it. First, figure out what it takes. Then we'll figure out a way to do it better."

"You'd do that for me?"

"If it will save you from our uncle."

Pumpkin crawls next to my leg and curls up. I absently pet her head. "I guess I could volunteer for the rescue here. I already know them since I used to foster. Maybe they'd let me work in the office."

"Perfect. Give them a call." He stands up. "Now let me be uncle to your brood while you get ready to head into town. I have some kittens to spoil at the pet store."

I slowly uncurl my legs to avoid disturbing Pumpkin.

He's right. If I'm stuck here, I should work my connections. Would I let Axel fund a rescue?

As I run a brush through my hair, I wonder if that's necessary. Maybe once I see the inside, I can figure out how to make this work.

32

DALTON

Is this long-distance thing working?

I don't know how to tell. It's been two weeks. I've had a hell of a schedule, so the phone calls and texts have been fewer.

Are we fizzling?

I hope not.

I'm alone in the cafeteria. Fitz has another surgery assist. She's winning the race on racking up time with her specialty.

Harrington knew going in that he wanted orthopedics, and he's setting a femur at the moment. Dude got all giddy about a broken bone. Unlike the patient, I'm sure.

The line of windows let in the bright sunshine of a glorious fall day. There was the tiniest nip this morning when I got in my Jeep. My first California winter is coming. Not that it will be a big change in temperature. That's the glory of SoCal.

I stick my spoon in my empty soup cup. I shouldn't

have bought lunch from the line, but lately I've been unmotivated to meal prep and bring my own. Mom found another job, averting a total disaster, but I still had to intervene with her apartment since she wouldn't get her first paycheck in time.

I press the heel of my hand into my eye. It's all such a grind. The texts and rare phone calls when my days off line up with Nadia's free time aren't enough to stave off the loneliness and drudgery.

At least, not today.

My phone buzzes. I'm almost glad to have a reason to go back to the ER. Better than sitting here brooding.

But the message says, "Visitor at the main desk."

For a second, my heart leaps, thinking it might be Nadia. She never came here before. Did she want to surprise me?

But it can't be. She texted a photo of the snow-capped mountains this morning. And she was heading to a rescue later to volunteer. Her first day.

She wouldn't fake all that.

Mom is on the other side of the country waiting tables. Hopefully.

Everyone else I know in LA is on shift with me.

I drop my cup in the trash and stride quickly through the rotunda to the dome of the main entrance. The visitor's desk is a huge round counter with two attendants and a security guard.

Quite a few people stand around it, but no one I recognize. Maybe this is random. A salesperson. Someone trying to recruit me. I don't know. I'll get rid of them.

Then I hear my name.

"Dalton."

I whirl around. It's Max, Nadia's deli cousin, big and intimidating in a sweatshirt and jeans. People move around him like a current, eyes on his build. I look like a kid in comparison.

Why would he come here? My stomach drops. Is something wrong with Nadia?

I have to force my voice out. "Everything okay?"

"Yeah." Max aims his thumb at a line of chairs. "You got a sec?"

"I do. But it might end at any moment."

"Understood."

We sit in the seats with an empty between us. Max barely fits between the arms. "I wanted to talk to you about Nadia."

Hell. Is he here to break up with me on her behalf? To warn me away from her? Wait. Does he even know? I won't make any assumptions again, not after I accidentally outed her in the bar bathroom as having a roommate.

I keep a straight face. "Is she doing okay?"

He shakes his head. "Did she really take in five extra cats?"

His tone is light. I force myself to relax. "Yeah. She's a rescuer at heart."

"She didn't even ask if she could come back and live with us." He stares at his hands, as if this is something that's bugged him.

"She didn't want to make Camryn deal with the allergy. It's a lot of cats."

Max leans back in his chair. "My head chef noticed her singing a ways back."

This is random. "Nadia was singing?"

"Yeah."

"She doesn't normally sing?" I don't know why I ask. I already know. Nadia wasn't a singer when I met her. It started … after. After we got together. She was lighter somehow. She smiled more.

"Not in the least. Her family is more serious than mine overall. My mom was a singer, Nadia's aunt Pat." His jaw twitches.

"Your parents include this Uncle Sherman she talks about, right? The one who wants her to work for the Pickles?"

Max nods. "Dad is kind of larger than life. Anyway, that's not what this is about."

But I'm not quite going to let this go. Max may not even know how Nadia feels about working with the other Pickles. "She said your dad wants her to work in the family business."

"He wants all the Pickles in it, yes. But it's not mandatory."

"She thinks it is."

He frowns. "He'll always make a place for a Pickle."

"Even if they don't want it?" I hope I'm not doing something out of turn, but maybe I can help Nadia. Max seems reasonable about this. Maybe something I will say can take the pressure off.

"Is that your opinion?" His expression darkens. I've walked into dangerous territory.

My phone buzzes. Damn. I'm out of time. I glance at it.

Booker: Head to curtain six.

She'll mean now. "I only have a quick sec."

Max leans forward. "The reason I brought up singing is because we all wondered if you were more than a roommate to Nadia. Her behavior has been, well, different."

He waits for a moment to see if I will confess.

Nope. I'm not giving up a single thing. Not this time.

Finally, Max grunts. "I see you're not going to talk about it." He stares me down, and dude, he's intimidating. It's like he's Thor, ready to beam you with his hammer.

I decide to evade. "I'm not sure what you mean."

"She's pulled out of the family business, and here you are spouting off about how she doesn't want it."

Ah. He's finally put that together. "She's happier volunteering at the rescue."

His eyes narrow. "So, you are still talking to her?"

"Why wouldn't I?"

"I don't know. A random roommate she barely knew. Then started singing about. Who are you, exactly?"

Now I'm mad. "Someone who cares about her. She didn't want to leave."

"She was never meant to live in LA."

"She liked it here."

"She's easily the smartest Pickle. She has an MBA." His voice is practically a growl.

"I know that."

He glares at me again. He's looking at me like I'm the bad guy. Am I? Am I holding Nadia back?

"What are you looking for from me?" I ask.

Max sighs and runs his hands through his hair. "I'm asking you, whatever hold you have on her, let her be. If she comes back to you, fine, whatever. But her brother is helping her get her dream. The family has her back. Whatever has made her hide what she's doing and who she's doing it with…" He fixes me with another oriented stare. "Can't be good for her."

He's right. Nadia kept secrets. But she felt she had to.

My phone buzzes.

Harrington: Booker's looking for you. Get down here.

I stand up. "You've made your point."

"All right." He doesn't stand or try to stop me as I head into the bowels of the hospital.

The Pickles protect their own.

33

NADIA

One of my favorite sounds is entering the cat sanctuary at the rescue.

Mews, big and little. Purrs, rumbles, the soft pad of cat feet landing on the hardwood floor as they jump from their perches to greet me.

I kneel with a new bag of toys, courtesy of Axel. The cats swarm me, running their sleek bodies along my legs, hoping they will get first dibs.

"Jolly, I brought you a new banana. Don't destroy it for at least five minutes." I give a jumbo orange cat the fabric banana stuffed with catnip.

Harold, an elderly Siamese, jumps onto my lap.

"I didn't forget," I tell him, pulling out a small mouse with rubber ears, his favorite.

He snaps his teeth around the colorful ear and takes off for a quiet corner.

The others are far less particular. I dump the rest of the toys on the floor. The cats are an undulating clump of fur, some choosing an item and dashing off with it, others turning up their noses and returning to their spots in the sun.

Pearl, a shiny white Persian with blue eyes, makes a bed out of the remaining pile and spreads out over it.

I stroke her long fur for a moment. "Time to visit the dogs," I tell her.

Several cats fix beady glares at me at that, as if they understand the word.

"Don't worry, you're all still my favorites."

I slide carefully through the door to make sure nobody escapes and head to the noisier end of the rescue building. I hear the yips and barks of the dogs before I reach the room. It's feeding time, so everyone is in their kennels for the moment.

Kendall, the primary caretaker of the dogs, will feed them and then release them back out to the yards, where they spend most of their day. They have several outdoor play areas. One for big dogs, one for small ones, one for puppies and injured dogs, and another for shy dogs who are too afraid to engage with the energetic ones.

I'm here to feed a new litter that was dumped near a campground and found by some hikers. They are little, and like my cat family at home, the mom was overburdened trying to keep them alive when already starving herself.

Kendall is busily measuring out bowls of food at the long counter on the side wall. She has her baseball cap on backward, and her jeans are muddy as usual. She likes to play with the dogs in the yards. "Heyo, Nadia," she says. "The formula's already in the warmer."

"Thank you!" I call. I collect the first bottle and

head to the sick bay where the mom and her puppies are living until they are better. It's a warm, cozy crate set on a counter, so it's easy for us to access the doggies who are in recovery.

Mom is a dachshund and Yorkshire terrier mix with a curly gold coat. There's no telling what the father was, but the babies are all over the place. One is a curly haired dachshund like mom. Two are more traditional dachshunds with long bodies and short brown hair. The fourth is hard to characterize. It's gray and chubby, with the same long nose as its siblings but a short body with more normal sized legs.

Kendall peers around me. "I still say the gray one is a totally different litter."

"Might be. At least the mom accepted it." I pull one brown puppy out and sit on a stool to feed it the bottle. It pulls hungrily at the formula.

"We should name them soon. Get them on the website." Kendall expertly fills an arm with six bowls of kibble, like a server at a high-end restaurant.

"I call this one Brownie in my head," I tell her.

"We could name them all after cookies," she says. "Clever names get them adopted fast." Then she's off to slide the bowls into the kennels.

Brownie finishes his bottle off quickly and drops off to sleep. I carefully set him in with the others and pull out the curly-haired one.

"Who should you be?" I ask her, taking a second bottle out of the warmer. "Blondie? Gingersnap?"

Ginger-Blondie snaps at the bottle like it's an enemy before finally settling down to drink. She's feisty, wriggling and squirming and getting formula everywhere.

"Good thing you're cute," I tell her, then feel the familiar warm wetness on my leg that means she peed on me, too. Rescue work is never glamorous.

I reach for a towel and tuck it under her to limit the fluids all over me until we're done. By the time I get her fed, then her two siblings, I'm overdue to work in the office.

Kendall is ushering the big dogs out to the play yard as I pass.

"You need help?" I ask her.

"Nah, Jake and Elmer are on the way for their shifts. I'll wait on them to let out the others."

I nod and head into the administrative part of the building.

I'm glad for all the work. Since I started helping, I've worked ten-hour days, five or six days a week. It's been good to keep my mind off Dalton and LA.

My chest tightens at the thought of him. We seemed so perfect. But maybe that's not enough. Circumstances have to work out, too.

Emily looks up from her desk as I enter the main room. Her bright red oversized cat's eye glasses are topped by a shock of wild gray hair sticking up in all directions. She's eccentric and funny and exactly the person you'd expect to be running a rescue.

Hers is based in an old rambling house outside Boulder. The cat room is a sunroom, added after the fact. The kennels are in the old garage, which has been expanded to triple its size.

The main office is the original living room, with the wall knocked out to incorporate the dining room into the space. The kitchen is intact, as it always was, with a table for the crew to eat lunch.

One bedroom is an intake room where we isolate new arrivals until they are assessed. The second bedroom houses all the accounting and paperwork storage. It has a desk, and I'm often in there making calls to donors and veterinarians and prospective foster homes.

She stands up to hold out a stack of folders. "Nadia, I'm so glad you're here. We're doing reports to keep our 501(c)(3) status active. You should learn about this. Warning—it's boring as hell."

I laugh. "I was warned about boring as hell in grad school."

Emily nods. "Good. I'm fairly sure we fall under the cutoff for filing the long form, but I need you to run the numbers since Mrs. Crabshaw, God rest her lovely soul, left us that money in her will."

I flip through the folders. "What's our fiscal year?"

"September to August."

"Got it."

The phone rings, and Emily plunks back down to grab it. "Boulder Fur Babies Rescue, this is Emily."

I tuck the folders under my arm to head to the sanctuary of the back room. Emily's voice can carry a country mile, and I have some focusing to do.

Even so, when I open the folder, the first thing I see is a receipt from a donor named Dalton Scout, an octogenarian who runs the ice cream shop downtown.

My finger runs across the name.

Dalton.

I've been gone almost a month. Our texts have gotten fewer. In fact, a week ago, they slowed to almost nothing. It's like the faucet shut off.

I should be getting over this.

But I'm not.

And I don't know what to do about it.

34

DALTON

The only way to get through this is to work.

I take on every case I can. Fitz and Harrington are more scarce anyway, having figured out their strengths and securing mentors.

I'm still flailing in the ER, which is fine. I can stick with emergency medicine if I want. It's what I put down in med school when I had to choose a direction, sort of de facto choice for the undecided. From here, I could be a general practitioner or go with internal medicine or any number of places.

But I feel lost.

It's been four days since I spoke or texted with Nadia, the longest we've gone.

I would never ghost her, and I don't want to let her go. But I am letting her take the lead. If she slows down, I slow down. I haven't forgotten what Max said. If she comes back to me, fine, but not to push her.

I hate long distance. Hate that she had to go. Hate that she can't find her way back.

But I don't hate that she loves her rescue work. Her MBA is helping them. They're straightening out their books, cutting costs, adding services, and streamlining. She's organizing a fundraiser to get more donors.

She's killing it.

They'll never let her go. Why would they?

She has so many options. She can stay at the rescue. She can become a consultant to rescues. She can fundraise. She can start her own rescue. The last thing we talked about in depth was how her brother Axel might set up a foundation for one.

And here I am, a doctor, sure, but unable to so much as decide on a specialty. I'm rudderless, just getting through each day.

"Hey, intern."

I pause outside the records room where I am supposed to be delivering files. I turn to see Dr. Frazier in his long white coat waving me down.

I set the records inside the door and close it. "Yes?"

"I've got a panicky pregnant woman in curtain six. She's having Braxton-Hicks. You know what those are?"

I try not to be insulted. I almost never work with Frazier. "Yes, early non-labor contractions."

"Right. She's convinced she's about to have the baby. Can you sit with her until the obstetric consult comes down? She's freaking out."

"Sure."

He passes me an iPad. "Here's her info."

I take it and head to the curtains, pulling up her records as I walk. I hesitate outside number six. Jennifer Martin, LMP Mar 9. That would make her roughly seven months along. That seems early for Braxton-Hicks.

"Knock, knock," I say, then slide through the part.

Jennifer sits alone on a bed, her face red, tears dripping onto her blue maternity dress.

"Jennifer Martin?" I ask.

She nods.

"What's your date of birth?"

"April 6, 1998."

"Perfect. How are you feeling?"

"The same. Lots of pressure. Lot of pain." She runs her hands along her belly.

"I'm Dr. Murphy. We have obstetrics coming down the first chance they can. I'm here to sit with you and monitor your progress."

"Okay." She gulps another sob. "I just … I lost my first one."

I frown and flip through the record. "I don't have that here."

"I told the nurse."

"How far along were you last time?"

"Ten weeks. They said it wouldn't happen again."

"You're much farther along this time. It won't be the same."

Her voice shakes. "Are you sure?"

"A first trimester miscarriage is very different from being in your third trimester." I try to give her a reassuring smile. "Is this the hospital where you plan to deliver?"

"No, I'm from Sacramento. I was here for a work

trip when the pain started. My husband is driving down, but it takes six hours."

I pull up a stool next to her. "That's scary. All alone in LA. Did you call your OB/GYN back home?"

"I did. The on-call nurse told me to come to the ER."

"Good call. How long have you been in pain?"

"Since about—" She cuts off to let out a long slow groan.

I feel uneasy. That seems like more than Braxton-Hicks to me.

"I feel something!" she cries. "Right now! I feel something."

Shit. I step to the curtain and peer out. "Nurse?"

There's no one at the moment.

I guess I better examine her myself. I've been present for three deliveries, so I know the basics, if that's where we are. I snatch up a box of gloves and put on a pair.

"It's coming!" Jennifer starts panting. "I knew it was real!"

It's my job to be confident and reassuring. "Let's see what we have."

I help her slide back and lift the skirt of her dress. Her underwear is soaked, tinged in pink.

We work together to pull down the underwear. Her hands are shaking.

The minute I take a closer look, I know I'm about to do a delivery. The head is crowning. We are out of time.

"Jennifer, I can see the baby's head. We've got this."

"It's too early!" she cries. "I'm not due for six more weeks."

"This is an excellent hospital," I tell her. "Everything is all right. See if you can huff without pushing."

If I can slow her down, I can get help in here, a nurse. Call the NICU team down. Right now, I don't dare step away until I see if it's coming immediately.

"Deep breath. Don't push. Huff through this contraction."

But I can already see it's too late. More fluid gushes out as the head emerges.

"Okay, Jennifer, we're having a baby. Go ahead and push." I place my hands into position to support the newborn.

She lets out a long, heavy groan, and the head comes fully out. I don't have suction. I don't have anything, but I use the paper sheet to wipe the baby's face and pull mucus.

"One more good push."

I shift the shoulders as Jennifer strains. Then he's out in my hands. A boy. Good grief, I don't have a blanket. I have nothing.

He's not crying. I flip him onto my arm and rub his back.

"Why isn't he crying?" Jennifer breathes in gulping sobs.

I aim his head down and rub again. The baby gasps, then there it is, that first tentative cry.

"Oh, thank God." Jennifer reaches out her arms.

I help lower the shoulder of her dress to place the baby against her skin. "Let's cover him with your skirt until we can get you properly set up."

When the baby is in place, I dash outside of the

curtain. I grab the first nurse I see. "I need a neonatal team NOW. We just had a premature birth in curtain six."

"What?"

"Get the team."

She takes off, and I race to the supply closet, snatching a couple of blankets. Jesus Christ, we could not have been less prepared.

By the time I return with the blanket, another nurse is inside, talking on the phone. I cover Jennifer and the baby.

"I need to call my husband," she says.

"We will. We still have a lot to do," I tell her. "The placenta. Assessing the baby. But you did it. You did it, Mom."

"Thank you for believing me."

I don't think I had a choice, but I tuck the blanket more tightly around her.

The NICU team arrives with an isolette. The neonatologist, a tall man in blue scrubs, takes in my badge. "You're an intern. Who is the doctor on this?"

"Dr. Frazier wanted me to sit with her. We were waiting on obstetrics."

"Frazier left a woman in labor?" The man stares at me incredulously.

I watch another member of the team listen to the baby's heart. "He assumed it was Braxton-Hicks."

"Jesus Christ." He turns to the bed. "Mom, we're going to take this little guy for a few minutes to make sure he's all right. We'll wheel him right behind you as we go to the maternity floor."

"I want Dr. Murphy to go with us," Jennifer says.

The neonatologist glances over at me. "Dr. Murphy is in emergency."

"I want him. Please. Nobody else listened to me."

"I can go," I tell him. "I'm almost off shift, anyway. I'm happy to help."

The neonatologist watches me another moment. "Was this your first delivery?"

I nod.

"All right. You earned it. Come up with us."

Obstetrics arrives with a rolling gurney and the curtain is overcrowded. I'm about to leave when Jennifer calls, "Dr. Murphy, here, please!"

I move to the head of her bed.

"Please don't leave me," she says. She reaches for my hand.

We get her moved to the gurney, and our parade heads out of the ER and to the service elevator. Jennifer won't let go of me.

Dr. Crisp, the OB/GYN on call, stands next to me as we go up to maternity. She watches me over the top of a pair of narrow glasses. "I hear this was your first delivery. No staff. No supplies."

"No choice," I say.

"You handled it well." She glances at the woman's hand clutching mine. "And you earned her trust. Are you sticking to emergency medicine?"

"I've been on the general medicine route."

She lifts her eyebrows. "We lost a neonatology intern. Would you be interested? We could do a trial for a while, share you between wards. It wouldn't have to disrupt your internship, and you could move to residency as planned next year."

Would I? This is a rare chance to try a new field.

As we exit the elevator and pass the windows where another newborn is getting its first cleanup, I wonder. Is this where I'm meant to be?

And then the next thought comes.

What would Nadia think?

I want to ask her.

Maybe I will.

35

NADIA

Neonatology. Working with babies. Dalton sounds excited.

We haven't spoken in over a week, and it's such a relief to hear his voice. "How has it been so far?"

"It's so different from the ER. We have emergencies, but not fifty a shift."

"Is there less drama?"

"I don't know. Nobody gets stabbed, but man, expecting parents can be a lot."

I pull Pumpkin from my jeans leg. She's dug her claws in. "But moving specialties doesn't change anything else?"

"No, I'll still take my intern exams in a few months and hopefully move up to my residency."

"Makes sense." I was almost hoping the unexpected call with the change in his life might mean he could transfer.

"I just wanted to tell you. Tell someone."

Pumpkin bats at my fingers as I push her away from

my jeans. She's determined to latch on. "Yes, of course. I'm glad you're figuring it out."

"Speaking of which, I have to run. I'm about to go on shift."

"Good to talk to you."

He ends the call with no endearments. No declarations.

Are we just friends now? Two people who update each other occasionally?

My heart squeezes. Surely not.

I pick up a feather toy to play with Pumpkin. She is desperate for attention. Ferris and Doppy realize I'm waving the yellow menace and dash onto the bed to join the fray.

"You all do know it's not a real bird, right?" I laugh as I move it around, watching them lose their minds trying to catch the dancing toy.

The front door creaks open, and I pause to listen. A booming voice at the bottom of the stairs makes my heart speed up.

Is that who I think it is?

Oh, no.

I hop up to open my bedroom door. I can't see the front door from here. I slide along the wall like I did in high school when I was sneaking out and peer around the edge to look down.

Uncle Sherman.

He's here.

The kittens have all escaped and are hopping down the stairs. Pumpkin takes a tumble and I gasp, rushing after her.

"There she is," Sherman says. "I heard you had a cat crew."

I catch up to Pumpkin and inspect her for injuries. She fights to be put down.

"Yes, a whole litter."

Ferris has already reached the bottom and circles Sherman's pant legs. My uncle's not much of a cat person, so he just watches with amusement.

Mom glances up with concern as I slowly make my way down. "Sherman was in Denver and decided to drive up."

I shoot her a look that says, *and you didn't warn me?*

"He decided to surprise us," she adds.

Oh, I see.

He knew what he was doing.

"Too bad about losing your lease in LA," Sherman says, rubbing his hands together. "I assume that means you are free to head to Florida? I am going there myself later this week. We could make a jaunt of it. See your brother. Take a tour of Dougherty."

I look at Mom again. She shrugs. Nobody stands up to Uncle Sherman.

But I have to. "I'm doing work here that I like. I don't plan on leaving anytime soon."

"Oh, really?" Sherman heads to the living room and sits on one of the oversized chairs, frowning when Ferris leaps into his lap.

I hope the kitten sheds a million white hairs on his suit.

Mom and I sit on the sofa, quickly joined by the

other three kittens. Two curl up in her lap. Greyson chooses me.

"What sort of work is this?" Sherman asks. "Should I buy them out?" He gives a gruff laugh.

"An animal rescue."

Now he scoffs. "That's a money-bleeding proposition."

I lift my chin. "Sometimes it's not about money."

His eyes lock on mine. "I'm okay with that. But if the organization can't stay afloat, you'll never get anywhere."

"I'm thinking of starting my own ancillary company, more of a fundraising venture."

He nods. "I'm listening."

"Most of the rescues are understaffed and working with volunteers. They could use a more professional and streamlined flow of funding, access to big donors and not just local businesses."

"And you would assemble a team for this."

"Exactly. Like the big organizations for other causes that distribute funds for major illnesses or children's hospitals."

"I like it. Put me down for startup funds."

"Axel is providing the seed money."

Sherman slaps his knees, startling Ferris into leaping to the floor. "I'll double it."

Mom glances my way, lifting her brows.

I'm not dumb. I know money comes with strings. "And what would you want your role to be in the organization for your investment?"

Uncle Sherman stares me down. "Silent benefactor."

He stands up. "Caprice, you got some champagne? Probably beer, if I know you outdoor types. Let's drink to this. Get Axel over here. We'll use his people to draw up some papers."

I sit still, not sure I've heard all this right. This was just an idea two days ago. I haven't hashed out how any of it would work. Where I would be based. Who I would hire.

Is he serious?

I follow him to the kitchen. "So, no Dougherty, then?"

Sherman shrugs, opening the fridge. "They're doing fine. Follow your passions. That's what I want for all the Pickles."

"I'm an Armstrong," I tell him.

He pulls out a bottle of beer, peers at it, and pops the top. He raises it to me like a toast. "Every Pickle's a Pickle."

For the next few days, I figure out where it makes the most sense to base my organization. California seems like a good place with its access to wealth, but when I look into the laws and licenses, I'm not sure.

Maybe I can create it in one state but have a secondary location in LA? One glance at real estate prices for an office makes me rethink that as well.

Plus, what am I going there for? Dalton? Is that even a possibility?

I'm not sure it is.

Besides, I should be here, near the rescue I love. When I told Emily my plan, she told me I could absolutely base out of their offices until I got on my feet.

I don't know exactly what to do, so I do nothing. I keep the status quo, working in town, feeding my kittens, and slowly creating a corporate structure, bank accounts, and a business plan.

I'm not sure I'll find a way to make LA work.

Maybe it wasn't meant to be.

36

DALTON

The weeks become a blur. If I thought being an intern in emergency medicine meant long hours, I had no idea how much more of that I would have in maternity.

Here, when a high-risk pregnancy arrives, often in distress, we sit through labor, a c-section sometimes, and then the real neonatal work begins.

Unlike in the ER, where patients come and go quickly, with only a small percentage checking in and requiring follow up, our mothers and babies are here for days, sometimes weeks or more.

I learn to make decisions cold, but keep my words and actions warm. Bedside manner can completely change an outcome with a mother in distress. Unlike downstairs, where the ER interns are treated like imbeciles, which is fair, since the situations are so varied and vast, here, we quickly become indispensable.

Parents get attached to the doctors in this ward, and the nurses are cherished partners. The highs are very high, like when we get quadruples safely born and all can go home.

But the lows are worse than any I experienced in emergency.

Many nights, particularly the bad ones, I long to call Nadia, to hear her voice, to feel there is a tether to the regular world.

But the weeks keep passing, and the ties that bound us stretch farther and farther.

I question the bond I felt. How embarrassing to fall in love with her so quickly, so naively. We didn't even date, or go to movies, or do any of the normal things couples do.

She feels like a far-off dream.

One day in early November, I meet up with Fitz and Harrington for coffee before our shifts.

"We haven't seen you in forever," Fitz says, ordering for me and passing me a cup. "How are the babies in maternity?"

"Terrifying," I tell her. "It's a crisis all the time, but when they go home, it's the best."

Harrington nods. "Bones don't die, generally. Orthopedics has settled my nerves."

Fitz takes her coffee and we head to a table by the windows in the cafeteria. "Surgery is intense. Sometimes we are in there for twelve hours straight. I had to buy different shoes, get wrist guards. I never imagined having to stand in the same position holding an artery until my arms want to fall off."

I nod. "I never imagined holding a baby who weighs less than a pound."

We fall quiet.

"Intern exams coming," Harrington says, peering into his cup.

"We'll study together," Fitz says. "We'll pass, no problem."

"Have either of you thought about transferring to a new hospital after the internship year?" I ask them.

"No way," Fitz says. "That's hard to do."

"No," Harrington agrees.

I look over the cafeteria. It's early, so mostly nurses and hospital personnel wander about.

"Is this about the girl?" Fitz asks.

I shrug. "Not really. I think it's done."

"Long distance is hard," Harrington says.

Fitz nudges him, making her curls bounce. "Like you would know."

Harrington shrugs.

"Where would you apply?" Fitz asks. "It's a long shot that you'd find an opening somewhere for a first-year resident."

She's right. I looked at Boulder after I moved to neonatology, and the closest I could get to Nadia would be in Denver, about an hour away. There's a children's hospital there. But it's a huge long shot. Any interns already there would have first pick at the residencies.

My phone buzzes. Twins crowning. "Here we go," I tell them. "Let's plan some study sessions."

"And we can grab a burger again," Harrington says.

"All of us," Fitz adds.

"Definitely." I pick up my coffee and stride out of the cafeteria.

The room I'm headed to is closer to the main bank of elevators than the service one, so I push the button in the atrium.

"Dalton?"

I turn. It's Camryn, looking resplendently pregnant in a yellow jumpsuit.

"Hey." My gaze meets Max, who shoulders a duffel bag. "You two checking in? Are you in labor?"

"My water broke," Camryn says. "So here we are."

"On time? Early? Late?"

"I was due next week," Camryn says. "Close enough, I'm told."

The elevator dings, and we all step in. I push seven for maternity.

"Thanks," Camryn says. "Are you going where we are?"

I nod. "I've moved to neonatology."

"Will we see you?"

"Maybe. I sometimes come in on healthy babies, but it's more likely I'm brought in for support in more complicated cases."

"Then I hope I don't see you," Camryn says with a laugh. "But seriously, if there is a problem, can we ask for you?"

"Of course."

She takes Max's hand. "That makes me feel better."

We pause on two, and a man pushing a woman in a wheelchair gets between us.

I'm glad, because I'm dying to ask about Nadia, and I'm less likely to do so with an audience. I shouldn't do it. Especially not with Max right there.

But the couple gets off on three, and we're alone again.

"Nadia's fine, by the way," Camryn says. "I talked to her last week."

I finally can't hold back. "Is she coming to see you? She was going to help with the baby."

"All the Pickles are en route," Max says, his low voice rumbling in the small space. Is that a warning sound? Should I avoid her?

The doors open to our floor.

Camryn squeezes my arm. "I'll tell her to find you. Where do you tend to be?"

"In the NICU, but it's controlled entry. She can text me. I can stop by your room."

"You can stop by whether she's there or not. I love knowing you're here. You saved her in that bar. I haven't forgotten that."

I step out and let them go ahead. They pause at the nurse's station for directions. I head the opposite way to assist with the twins.

Nadia will be here.

Maybe today, if she drives.

I have a feeling that the minute I see her, I'll know what to do.

37

NADIA

When we get the call that Camryn has checked into the hospital, Mom and I quickly pack the car to drive to LA.

Dad stays behind with the cats. He holds Ferris and Doppelgänger as he says, "I've seen lots of babies. You ladies take care of Cam."

Mom's eyes tear up again. She keeps having bursts of crying. This is the first Pickle grandbaby on Uncle Sherman's side. She's in deep mourning for her sister, Aunt Pat, who isn't here to meet her first granddaughter. She died so young.

I drive through the desert, mostly holding Mom's hand. I know she's worried Max will be sad about his mom, and Uncle Sherman will be clueless without Pat to navigate this huge family moment.

"I'm going to be there for her," Mom says. "Cam's family isn't worth a damn. She doesn't have a mother figure anywhere."

She's right. There is a huge rift between Cam and

her family. She and her brother Franklin were close growing up, having to raise themselves with delinquent parents. Franklin was wildly overprotective and didn't want her dating anyone.

But then Camryn met Max. He was Franklin's best friend back then.

Things got tough when Franklin declared his sister off limits, leading to blows, and ultimately a disaster that forced Cam to cut her brother out of her life.

Now he'll be an uncle, if they can all mend the bridge. Uncle Sherman won't encourage it. Max might.

But regardless of what happens in Camryn's family, the Pickles are strong. "Granny Alma will be with us too," I tell her. "We're going to surround them with love."

Mom sniffs, pressing a tissue to her nose. "We will."

After ten hours of driving, we contemplate stopping for the night in Vegas, but Mom takes a driving shift. We arrive in LA around ten p.m.

"Should we go to the hospital?" Mom asks, gripping the wheel as we navigate the mostly empty highways.

"I have a key to their house if you want to sleep. The last update was that they expected the baby in the middle of the night." I've been texting with Max.

"That's a long labor," Mom says. "It only took six hours with you."

"What about Rhett? Do first babies take longer?"

She nods, glancing down at my phone for navigation. "He was eight."

"Cam is so tiny. I don't see how that baby can even be in there."

"It's amazing how we stretch." Mom exits, and I see we're heading toward South General.

Would Dalton be at the hospital? I haven't texted him to tell him that Camryn is there. Isn't he on the maternity ward now? I've only had scant details of his move to neonatology. I'm not clear if the NICU is on the same level as regular maternity. Probably. It would make sense.

What if I see him?

I probably look a fright. I pull down the mirror, blinking at the automatic light. My hair is all over the place, falling from the messy bun I shoved it into when we got the message that Cam's water had broken.

I didn't shower. I threw on a pair of sweats.

Why didn't I think this through?

I tug my hair down, but that's not much better. It cascades over my shoulders in a snarled mass, half straight, half crimped from the elastic band.

Mom glances over at me. "I don't think anyone will care how you look."

Right. Dalton was a roommate. I can't mention him.

I say the only thing I can think of. "Max will tease me."

"He'll do that no matter what."

That's true. All the cousins are close, but I've always had a special relationship with Max. It's one of the reasons I ran to his deli when I graduated, trying to avoid the Pickle empire.

And I'd done it. I'm well on my way to understanding the business model of animal rescues, and their expenses, their needs, how they operate.

I'm happy there. And I have the family's blessing.

I snap the mirror closed and throw my hair back into its messy bun. It's fine. I probably won't see him, anyway.

We pass the entrance to the ER, and I can picture Dalton standing out there, opening the door of the car he called after my bar debacle. It seems so very long ago.

Mom turns into the garage, and I have to bite my lip to stem the flood of emotion. I want to see him. I will see him. It would be wrong not to see him while I'm here.

I jerk my hair down again and rake my fingers through it. I have lip gloss in my bag. I can tidy up. There will be hours to wait.

And it's not like Dalton and I went on fancy dates or dressed up for each other. Our entire relationship had been built on our shared apartment. Regular meals. Watching television. Playing with cats.

This is the version of me he knew best.

I slide the elastic on my wrist. "You ready for this?" I ask Mom.

She nods, also dropping her mirror to look at herself. "I cried off my mascara."

"I never had any to begin with."

She rubs her finger under her eyes and grins. "Good thing we're not walking any red carpets while we're here."

"You never know."

She flips up the visor and kills the engine. "I'm glad we came together."

"It's going to be so great. A girl! A little girl Pickle."

She laughs. "Every Pickle's a Pickle."

We head inside, navigating the labyrinth of the hospital as we follow the signs to the elevators.

Seventh floor. As we go up, I wonder if Dalton takes this elevator, or if there is one for doctors that he uses. There's no mirror in here, so I can't judge what I look like in my sweats, all stretched out from the drive.

It's fine.

We step out of the elevator immediately opposite the glass windows of the nursery. Only one newborn is in there, red-faced and crying as he's cleaned by a nurse. Four gray-haired family members stand close together, filming every moment with their phones.

Mom slides her arm through mine. "This is a happy place."

"I think that baby in there might disagree."

She laughs. "It's a big shift from a watery slumber to the real world."

"Is it too late for me to go back in?"

She laughs. "If only I could keep you that close for always."

The nurse's station is empty, but I already have the room number. I point at a plate on the wall. "Room 739 is that way."

"Did you get an update since the last one?" Mom asks.

"No. It's been an hour."

"Oh, it would be so great if she's been born."

We hurry down the hall, passing a cluster of chairs

with a TV in the corner. I stop when I spot Uncle Sherman. "Hey!"

Mom turns to see who I'm talking to. "Sherman! What are you doing out here?"

"I got kicked out." He sits with his elbows on his knees, his hands tightly together.

I sit next to him. They might not want more visitors if things are intense. "How did you get here so fast?" Sherman lives in New York.

"Dell let me use his plane. Grammy came with me. She's in the room. Camryn doesn't want anyone else until it's done. She was struggling."

Mom sits on the other side of him. "Then we'll wait with you."

"Jason's on the way, flying up from Austin. He'll be here in a couple of hours. Anthony is driving up in the morning."

"I didn't even think to text him," Mom says. "We could have all come together."

"Anthony's not in Boulder at the moment," Sherman says. "There's a cooking event in Vegas. I told him to finish up and come tomorrow. Baby'll be here all the same."

"It will be nice to see all the boys," Mom says.

Uncle Sherman nods, his hands nearly white from his tight grip. His eyes are red. Has he been crying?

"I'll go get us all some coffee," I say. "It might be a long night."

Mom nods. She takes Sherman's hands.

I figure they might want to talk about Aunt Pat. I

hurry down the hall when a long, guttural cry from a nearby room startles me.

Whew. That's intense. I might stick with cats.

I keep going, assuming I'll find vending of some sort, eventually. Every hospital show I've ever watched has shown people getting coffee from a machine. There's bound to be one somewhere.

I turn a corner, surprised to see another bank of windows with a nursery. Did I make a circle?

But the baby and grandparents are gone. This one is darkened, with blinking lights on tall equipment among the rows of enclosed plastic beds.

The NICU.

There's a small glassed-in office with a nurse inside typing on a computer. She slides a window open when she sees me. "Visiting hours are nine a.m. to four. A parent will need to escort you."

"Oh, I'm just looking for coffee."

She smiles. "I see. There's a family station in every hall. It's marked with a sign. There's juice, snacks, and coffee for the laboring moms and their guests. You might have to check more than one to find a warm pot at this hour."

"Thank you." That's nice that they have stations for us.

I'm about to walk away, but I hesitate. The woman is about to close the window when she notices. "Did you need something else?"

"Do you know Dalton Murphy? I think he's an intern on this floor."

"Sure. Dr. D is very popular around here. The moms love him."

My heart swells to know he's doing well. "Is he here tonight?"

"Sure, he's in here. You want me to see if he's available?"

"Oh. I couldn't bother him."

But she's already getting up. She leaves through an interior door between her office and the NICU.

I walk past the secure door to the windows to watch her navigate the rows. There's an order to them. Closest to the door and her office are low, clear beds with wiggling babies. There are moms inside, rocking in chairs, some of them holding their infants.

But as she walks, the beds get more elaborate, with more machinery. There are parents there too, but none of them hold their babies. Some of the set-ups are elaborate with handmade signs and stuffed animals atop the machines.

My throat tightens. How hard it must be to live on such a knife's edge.

She stops, and I peer into the shadows through the glass.

Then I see him, surprised at how easily I recognize the shape of his frame, the movement of his stride.

I know the moment he sees me too, because his step falters, then he's closer, and I can make out his eyes above a mask.

He waves, and I wonder if he's stuck in there, locked in, if there is some procedure to keep it safe and germ free.

But then he pushes a button, and he's out in the hall. Dalton.

It's been less than two months, but it feels like a lifetime. He looks the same in light blue scrubs. He pulls down the mask to show his smile. He's scruffy, so it must be the end of a long shift.

And I'm so happy to see him. It all floods back at me.

Dalton. Our home. Our life. Our cat family.

I let out a cry, and there's no space for niceties. No "hello" or "How are you?" I'm in his arms, and he holds me tightly. Then I'm crying on his shoulder.

He doesn't ask questions or say anything at all. He just hangs on.

We remain a tight ball until I hear the slide of the glass again.

It's the nurse. "Dr. D, Jamie is about to come on shift. Why don't you go on home?"

"You sure?"

"Yeah, I'll tell Davison you've clocked out. We don't have any high-risk labors on the floor."

He pulls away and takes my hand. "Thanks, Amy." We walk along the halls. "Did your cousin have her baby?"

"Not yet."

"Do you want to check on her?"

"I was off getting coffee for family when I found the NICU in my wandering."

"I can help with that." He leads me to one of the family stations. "This is the good one. Angelica, one of the RNs, always keeps hot coffee in it."

We push through the door to the aroma of a French mocha. It's heavenly. Dalton lets go of me and starts pulling cups. "How many did you need?"

"Three. My mom is here. And Uncle Sherman."

"Oh, the hard one."

"Not so hard. He let me go."

Dalton fills each of the cups from the machine and caps them. "For the rescue? He approved?"

I realize how little we've talked lately. "Yes, he's signed on as an angel investor."

He hands me a cup. "Should we deliver these?"

"I … uh." I don't know what to say. My emotions are tumbling over each other.

Then our gazes clash, and I know he's feeling it, too. We both set down our cups, and this time when we come together, it's not an embrace but an unbridled kiss.

Our mouths lock together, our bodies pressed so hard I can feel the strings of my sweatpants pushing against my belly.

He tastes like coffee already, another hint at the length of his shift, and I take in everything about him like I've never known it, like I'm discovering him again for the first time.

Dalton and I lived together, slept together, and had many intimate moments.

But this is different. Desperate. Uncontrolled. He lifts me onto the counter, wrapping my legs around his waist.

I can't get enough of him, my hands gripping his shoulders, our tongues clashing. He rocks against me, and I curse my sweatpants, his scrubs. I want him with an ache I've never known before. It's not just an emotion, but a physical pain.

His hands slide beneath my sweatshirt, cupping my bra. He touches me as if he's dying, as if my skin is the only thing that stands between him and catastrophe.

Then the air changes, and a startled, "Oh!" breaks through.

I pull away.

The door has opened.

God. It's Mom.

My mom.

"Nadia?" She glances back at the door. "I thought you got lost."

Dalton steps back, tugging at the blue cap covering his hair.

Mom waves her hand toward the hall. "A nurse said you were in here…" she trails off.

I can't imagine what she thinks. That I jumped a hot doctor faster than a character in *Grey's Anatomy?*

I let out a long, slow breath. "This is Dalton."

Mom flashes an uncertain smile, but there's some relief there, too. Maybe she *did* think I jumped a random doctor. "The roommate?"

"Yes." I jump down from the counter and straighten my sweatshirt. This is too much.

"Nice to meet you, Dalton," Mom says. "I'm Caprice Armstrong, Nadia's mother."

At the word *mother*, Dalton takes another step back, but then he recovers. "Mrs. Armstrong, it's nice to meet you." He extends a hand. "You've met our kittens, then. The kittens. Uh, *Nadia's* kittens."

Yeah, he's nervous.

Mom looks back and forth between us. "I take it there was more than a roommate situation happening." She frowns. "It must have been hard, leaving, then."

I glance over at Dalton. His mouth is a tight line.

This conversation is for another time. "Is there any news on Camryn?"

Mom shakes her head. "Still in labor." She spots the coffee cups. "Were these ours?"

"Uh, yes." I pass her two of the cups. "I was, uh, about to head that way."

Now Mom bites back a smile. "Sure you were." She turns to the door, then realizes she can't open it with her hands full. "Dalton, do you mind?"

He leaps forward to get the door.

"I'm going back to Sherman," she says. "You know, it might make sense for you to get some sleep. Why don't you head out? I'll keep you updated."

"Okay," I say. "I guess I can go to Camryn's."

Mom glances back at the two of us. "Of course. *Camryn's.*" She says it like she knows dang well we'll head to our apartment. "I'll text you as things progress."

Then she's gone again.

Dalton pulls off his cap. "Well, that secret is out."

I turn to him. "It should never have been a secret. I don't know why I ever thought that was important."

He stands there, watching me, then tosses the paper cap in the trash bin. "I'm off. Are we going home?"

I draw in a deep breath. *Home.* "Yes. Please. Take me there."

And I do mean *take me.*

38

DALTON

We stumble through the door of the apartment, kissing the entire way.

When Nadia looks around the place as if to assess it for changes, I scoop her up and walk her to the bed.

She lets out a "Whoop" as I toss her onto Optimus Prime.

Then I'm over her, braced on my arms, looking down at her face.

I'm still in shock over that first glimpse I got of her through the NICU window. Even though I knew she would be back after talking to Camryn, I didn't expect to see her yet. She must have jumped in her car the moment she heard and drove straight to the hospital.

All the things I planned to do and say evaporated when we were breathing the same air. I need to touch her, to kiss her, to hang on.

And now that we're here, back in our space, I don't see how I can let her go again.

I press a long, lingering kiss on her mouth.

Her arms encircle my neck. The feel of her is a revelation, like I've arrived at true north. My hands won't stay still, caressing her cheek, her neck, grazing the side of her breast. I can't get enough.

The sweatshirt covers too much of her, so I lift the bottom and inch it up over her belly. Her skin is warm, and my fingers bump along her rib cage, my senses flooded with familiarity.

She breaks the kiss, breathing faster, her eyes on mine. I slip my hand beneath her bra, cupping the warm, soft breast. Her chest heaves as she sucks in a breath.

Slow. I'm going to take this so slow. I want none of this to end, and I will draw it all out as long as possible.

I move down her body to press my lips against the hollow beside her belly button. I make my way up, pushing the sweatshirt over her head.

As I reach the base of her bra, I reach behind her to unclasp the hooks.

She lets out a sigh as it releases. I tug it away.

Now she's all mine to worship, touch, and taste. I hold both breasts, kneeling over her, my tongue sliding around one nipple, then the other.

Her back arches, and I grip more tightly, eliciting a moan.

It feels like forever since I've seen her like this, and yet it is as familiar as yesterday. I continue the slow, thorough exploration of her body, then move one hand to the waistband of her sweatpants.

She squirms beneath me, eager for me to move on.

She seems to want more skin contact, because she tugs the shirt to my scrubs over my head.

The heat of our connection makes me rock hard, and it gets much harder to take things slow.

But I do, easing the sweatpants down her legs. They get stuck at her tennis shoes, but I pause a moment to untie them and toss them on the floor.

When her legs are bare, I work my way back up with excruciating patience, kissing the inside of her ankle, her calf, and the bump of her knee.

When I reach her thigh, she sucks in a breath. I hesitate inches from the edge of her panties, savoring the anticipation.

She wriggles again, needing me to move forward. And I oblige, slipping my fingers beneath the lace band to pull them down.

The scrap of satin falls to the floor without a sound. I grasp one of her knees and edge it aside. She's naked before me, spread wide, resplendent in the low light.

I want to memorize every inch of her. But right now, I want to please her, to make her cry out in the night. I use both thumbs to open her wide, and when my tongue makes its first long lick, she lets out a keening cry.

Her belly shudders, and I realize how pent up she's been. How much we both have been longing for each other. I slip a finger inside her and suck on the pronounced nub of her clit.

That's all it takes. She's over the top, grabbing my hair, crying out my name and random syllables and sliding into a lengthy, breathy groan.

Her body shudders, her hips rocking back and forth.

I keep licking, drawing it out, unrelenting, until she holds my head still.

We lie there for several heartbeats, letting her body settle. Then she pulls herself up to sitting and takes my arms, lifting me so that she can rid me of the pants.

She has the same problem, pausing to remove my shoes. Then I'm naked by the bed and she scoots backward, drawing me down on top of her.

When I enter her, she cries out again. Her eyes sparkle with tears. I'm emotional, too, clasping her head as I move inside her.

This is where we belong, where we should always be.

How can we get this back?

She wraps her legs around my back and moves up and down, wanting more speed, more depth. I give it to her, and the bed rocks as I take her hard and fast.

She gasps, a guttural cry escaping her a second time. I crash into her body, unrelenting, crazed. I need her like nothing else. I will do anything for her. Quit the hospital. Live in my car. I can't let her go again.

She grips my shoulders and I release into her, my whole body alight, dazzled and electric to be here again, making her mine, being hers.

I hold myself above her, trying to get my bearings.

She presses her face into the side of my neck like she always used to, and I drag her tightly against me. I want as much connection with her as I can get for as long as possible.

We roll onto our sides, listening to the silence of the room. It's never been so quiet when we were together, with cats padding around before.

I want them back too.

Eventually, our breathing slows and we both trace lazy circles on each other's skin.

"How long do we have until your next shift starts?" she asks.

"Tomorrow evening."

"Will you work twelve or twenty-four?"

"Twelve."

She breathes against my skin. The warmth of her is comforting. But she'll get a text soon. The baby will be born. She'll spend time with family. I'll have another shift.

I try to push the thoughts away, but they must be crashing down on Nadia as well, as she says, "I won't be staying to help like I originally planned when I lived here. I have work to do in Boulder."

Everything in me tenses. "So you'll leave again?"

Her eyelashes flutter against my jaw. "I don't want to." The way she looks up at me in the low light from the kitchen is so familiar that I half expect a kitten to suddenly squirm between us.

"What do we do?" I pull her even closer, as if I could draw her into me.

"Los Angeles is so expensive," she says. "I looked and looked. Unless I take a high-paying job in some soul-sucking corporation, I can't swing it."

"You mean renting a place for the cats?"

"I mean starting a rescue, or working with rescues. I've tried every which way."

I kiss the top of her head. "Then I will have to find a way to come to you."

"How? You're in a program."

"I can transfer after my intern year. I'll apply anywhere I can in Colorado."

She pulls away to look at me. "Is there a chance you'll get something?"

"I will do my absolute best."

"When will you know?"

"After I pass my exams. That's when we either get promoted in our current programs, or if we decide to go in a different direction, we do a new internship somewhere else."

"Would you have to intern again if you move?"

It's likely, but I don't say that. "I'll do my absolute best."

"Okay," she says. "Until then, I'll come back to LA more often. The cats are doing great at my parents'."

"If I get even forty-eight hours off, I'll come to you."

She lets out a laugh. "When does that happen?"

"Pretty much never."

She tucks her head back against me. "I'll visit. I should have already."

"We'll figure it out," I tell her. "Now that we know."

"What do we know?"

"That it was more than something convenient. That it's real."

She presses her cheek to my shoulder. "Do you still love me?"

She's looking away, as if she is afraid of the answer. "I didn't know until I saw you. And it's definitely, undeniably, yes."

She can't look at me, but her words shake me to the core. "I think maybe I'm starting to love you, too."

Everything in my body relaxes, as if I've finally come to the top of the mountain after a long, difficult climb.

I turn her face to mine. "You make me the happiest man alive."

"Even if I get us kicked out of apartments?"

"I'll take in kittens with you each and every time."

She lifts her chin to press her lips to mine. We're mid kiss when her phone buzzes across the room.

We both sit up. "The baby!"

Nadia lunges for it, quickly scanning the screen. "She's here! Just now!"

I scramble for a pair of jeans. "Let's go."

"But you need sleep!"

"What's a few more hours?"

We hustle into our clothes and dash for the car.

We have a new Pickle to meet.

39

NADIA

Everyone is assembled in Camryn's room when Dalton and I make it back to the hospital.

"You chose the right time to return," Mom whispers. "They just brought baby Esmee back from her exam and cleanup."

I grip Dalton's hand as Grammy Alma takes the baby out of the clear crib and walks around the room to show her off.

It's almost two a.m. but no one looks tired, other than maybe Camryn, who sits against the pillows with her hands propped on another pillow over her belly. She seems peaceful, though, watching everyone's reaction to meeting Esmee.

Jason arrived while I was gone, and he and Uncle Sherman stand near Max. It'll be nice when Anthony arrives tomorrow. I haven't seen all three of my cousins together in a long time.

Sherman glances at me, raising his eyebrows when he spots my hand joined with Dalton's.

I turn away, watching Grammy show the baby to Mom.

Mom brushes a finger across the stretchy pink and blue striped hat. "Hello, little Esmee."

Then Grammy steps before us. I tilt my head and peer at the baby's solemn slate-blue eyes. She's quiet and seems thoughtful and wise. Maybe babies really do have all the knowledge of the world when they arrive.

"Hello, Esmee," I tell her. "I'm going to spoil you!"

This gets a gentle round of laughter from the room.

Grammy moves to Jason, who twiddles her nose, then shows off his thumb hidden in his fist. "Let the record show that I was the first to steal her nose!"

Another round of laughter. My chest feels full to bursting with pride and love. This is what it feels to have family. To stay up all night to meet a new member. To celebrate with quiet joy. I glance at Dalton. He has so little, like Cam.

Uncle Sherman takes the baby from Grammy. "Welcome, my first granddaughter," he says. "Your Grandma Pat would be so proud." The catch in his voice, coming from such a big, burly, gray-haired man, causes several of us to tear up.

"Pat is here," Grammy says. "Of course she is. How could she not be watching over this angel?"

Sherman lifts the bundle to his face to place a kiss on the baby's forehead. Then Max turns to him to take the baby and return her to Camryn.

There are rounds of photos and videos. Then we filter out, leaving the parents some privacy with their new baby.

We all stand in the hall, whispering our goodbyes.

Jason shakes Dalton's hand. "I didn't realize Nadia was seeing someone."

"You're all the way in Texas," I tell him. "You don't keep up."

Mom side eyes me at that, and Uncle Sherman rocks back on his heels.

"Well, I think he's perfectly handsome," Grammy says. "Do you live in Boulder, too?"

I glance at Dalton.

"I'm an intern at this hospital. I met Nadia while she was living in LA."

"Oh, so you two are apart right now." Grammy's smile wavers.

"We'll figure it out, Grammy," I tell her.

Our group walks toward the elevator.

"Sherman, where are you staying?" Mom asks.

"Grammy and I are at a hotel a couple of blocks away," Sherman says. "We'll be back early in the morning."

"Are you going to stay at Max's house?" Grammy asks her. "You might need to go back in the room to ask for a key."

"I have one," I tell her.

"Oh, good." She pats my hand. "Always planning ahead, aren't you, sweet Nadia?"

We crowd into the elevator.

"Dalton, what sort of intern are you?" Grammy asks.

"I'm in neonatology," he says. "I work in the NICU."

"How lucky for us!" Grammy exclaims. "Oh, Nadia, you should marry this one, and quick!"

My cheeks burn and Dalton squeezes my hand.

"But, however will you to get back together?" Grammy looks between the two of us.

Sherman clears his throat. "We're founding a business for Nadia. It can have branches anywhere."

"What kind of business?" Grammy asks.

We reach the bottom floor, and Sherman holds open the door.

"An animal rescue," I say right as Sherman answers, "A charitable organization."

Grammy chuckles. "A charitable animal rescue. How delightful."

We walk through the quiet atrium.

"I'll see you all tomorrow, or I guess, later today," Jason says.

"Come to Max's with me," Mom says. "Nadia, can you give me the key?"

"Nadia's not going with you?" Grammy asks.

Everyone looks at me, and my cheeks heat again.

"I'll be back up here later," I tell everyone, fishing my keys out of my bag. "Here, Mom. You take the car. I came with Dalton anyway."

"Oh, I see," Grammy says with a twinkle in her eye. "Young love. So fantastic." She threads her arm through Sherman's. "Let's get an old woman some shut-eye. I expect everyone back here before lunch!"

We break into pairs, Mom with Jason, Uncle Sherman with Grammy, and me with Dalton.

"That was a big dose of Pickle," I tell him. "You okay?"

"Easier than meeting your mom while I have you pinned to a counter," he says.

"You'll never live that down at gatherings," I warn him.

"I figured." We walk out into the cool Los Angeles air. "I like your family. It's so big and full of personalities."

"You haven't met the half of it. Did you know one of my cousins married a prince?"

"Oh, so I'm getting into royalty?"

I like how we're talking about a future even though there is so much to figure out.

"The royalty is about seven places removed." We walk across the staff parking lot to Dalton's Jeep. "But the Avalonions treat the Pickles like family. There's no disdain. No royalty on your side?"

He scoffs as we pass under a lamp. "I don't have much of anything at all. My dad's parents passed a long time ago. I never really knew them. My mom, well, you know about her. Her dad is long gone. Her mom is in a nursing home in Georgia."

"Do you have aunts and uncles? Cousins?"

"I think so, but I don't know them. Dad had a brother who married a woman abroad where he was stationed and never returned to the states. Mom has a sister somewhere. Florida, maybe."

"So there could be a whole league of them about."

"Maybe." He unlocks the Jeep, and I climb into the

passenger side, fixing a duck that has turned sideways. It's an Elvis.

"I bet we could find them. Do some traveling once your schedule is better. Meet some Murphys."

He starts the engine. "You make it sound so easy."

"It doesn't have to be hard. You're not asking anything from them. Just a meeting. If they suck, you don't visit them again."

He turns around the back out of the slot. "It's quite possible they all suck."

"I think it's worth finding that out. Who knows? By the time we get serious, maybe you'll have a whole slew of Murphys to invite to a hypothetical wedding."

His eyes meet mine. "A wedding. That's a nice thought. You sure you know me well enough to consider that as part of your future?"

"I know the important things."

We pause at the exit, not yet pulling out onto the street. The night is quiet, the lamps glowing over an empty bus stop.

"What are the important things?" he asks.

"That you love my cooking."

"I do."

"That you don't hog the covers."

"Unless you try taking Optimus Prime."

I laugh. "That you take care of our space and the creatures in it, even when they aren't allowed to be there."

He reaches for my hand and lifts it to kiss my knuckles. "Our home is worth whatever it takes to keep it happy and safe."

I hesitate a moment, my head rushing with what I want to say next. But then I just do it. "And I know I love you, Dalton. I think I knew it before, but it seemed illogical. Too fast. Too nontraditional. It didn't fit the usual order of meeting, and dating, and learning each other little by little."

He kisses my hand again. "I think that's why it happened so fast. We skipped the boring parts."

I laugh again at that. "It has never been boring."

He leans across the space between us. "I've loved you since the moment I realized we were fighting for the same apartment."

I shake my head. "Not possible."

He reaches out for my chin and lifts it so our gazes meet. "I think love is a seed. But it's not a given that it will grow. It takes the right environment. Nurturing. Care. But I think it can be planted from the very beginning. And I feel certain that seed arrived the moment you turned around in that chair at the first apartment office."

He might be right. Each moment was another sprout. Accepting Catzilla. Helping with dinner. Pickle jokes. Romance novels. Taking in the kittens. It grew as our lives intertwined.

I lean in the rest of the way. As our lips brush against each other, that spark hits me as it always did. Two bodies. Brain chemistry.

A match.

I have every faith we are going to figure this out. Cities. Hospitals. Rescues. Where to put our kittens.

There is no falling apart. Only growing together.

EPILOGUE: NADIA

Eight months later.

The ducks on the dash bounce as we leave the asphalt highway for a dirt road.

I lean forward to keep them from falling to the floor.

Dalton glances my way. "We're going to have to tape them down!"

"We might."

A yellow one covered in hearts, which I left for him this last Valentine's Day, escapes my hands and dives into the cup holder.

"Two points!" Dalton calls.

The road smooths out as we drive alongside pasture land, the mountains in the distance. It's a vividly bright summer day, and flowers spread across the lowlands like yellow stars.

I hang on as we bounce over another rut. "Maybe we can put down some gravel there to fill it in," I tell him. "Or we can see if there is room in the budget to pave it."

We drive another minute or so before the sprawling house appears, surrounded by trees. The property used to be a ranch, decades ago, but it's being sold by the retired couple who has owned it for fifty years.

I reach out to hold Dalton's hand. "You think they'll let it go?"

"I hope so."

The couple has been reluctant to sell, taking the property on and off the market multiple times over the last five years. They wanted one of their kids to take it over, but none of them has been willing.

We approach the main house. Behind it looms a large hay barn, and beyond it, a long pole barn meant to house cattle when necessary. There are almost a hundred acres attached to the parcel, some five hundred getting sold off over the years as the operation slowly shut down.

We toured it a few weeks ago with the real estate agent, but today we meet the family. We have been warned this is the make-or-break moment.

Another couple stands off to the side of the house, not much older than us. The man points out at the mountain view, then lifts a fancy camera to take a photo.

"Do we have competition?" I ask. "I thought we were the only ones who put in an offer."

Dalton kills the Jeep. "Maybe someone else stepped up yesterday or today."

My heart speeds up. We can't lose this place! It's the best option for the rescue operation, I imagine. A place not just for dogs and cats, but horses and goats and even exotic pets, at least until proper placements can be found for them.

There would be a veterinary office where we saw paying patients, boarding to help with costs. I had it all worked out how it could be profitable!

Dalton squeezes my hand. "Don't worry. We're going to charm the pants off these people. You've planned every little thing."

"I wish we weren't competing. I hate competing."

He kisses my knuckles. "We're going to win."

"We have to. It's only thirty minutes from the Children's Hospital, and forty minutes from Denver." It's also near my brother Court and their goat farm.

It's so perfect. I can't bear to lose it.

"Let's go get it." Dalton releases my hand.

"Maybe we can scare the other couple off. Tell them it's haunted."

Dalton laughs as we exit and meet in front of the car. "I think I've seen this episode of Scooby Doo."

"It's every episode." I watch the other couple out of the corner of my eye as we approach the front door. We haven't even made it to the porch when it opens.

Stan Velmont, the owner, gives us a wave, motioning for his wife to come out with him.

We all shake hands.

"Nice to finally meet you," Dalton says. "I'm Dalton, and this is Nadia."

"He's a doctor," I blurt out. "For babies. He saves babies."

I don't miss the way Dalton tries to hide his smile. "And she rescues animals."

Yeah, we're pulling out all stops, just like the first time.

It's kind of nice that we're doing it together.

"That's what we hear," Stan says. "You want to turn it into an animal rescue."

"It's a lovely idea," his wife Maria says. "Will you put more buildings on the property?"

The other couple walks our way. I feel like I must state our case before they can get their claws in.

"We plan to build a state-of-the-art veterinary clinic," I tell her. "The existing buildings will be used for boarding. We think mixing pets with families with the ones up for adoption will help all of them, plus give the needy ones more visibility among pet owners who might take them in."

"You have experience with this?" Stan asks.

It feels like a job interview. "Of course," I say, noticing that the other couple has paused at the edge of the porch, a good twenty feet away. Time for closing arguments.

"I have volunteered for a rescue in Boulder for years and this last year helped fund an expansion. I have put together all the seed money necessary to create a more broadly based operation, plus I have the support of an entire community of veterinaries, rescue volunteers, and my personal family, as I've lived in the area much of my life."

Maria holds up a hand. "I believe you. I think you are a bright young woman. And of course, we already know about Axel and Court. The Pickles are a beloved part of the Boulder community."

"And that hotel," Stan says. "Fancy, fancy."

I glance at Dalton. "It is beautiful."

"Come on in," Maria says. "We should sit down."

Maria leads us into a living room. "Did you know Stan and I got married right here on the property? He carried me right over the threshold after."

"That's lovely." But even as I say it, I worry. Will they be traditional? Dalton and I aren't married. He's only recently moved to Boulder after his internship.

He got a resident position at the Children's Hospital in Denver in a direct swap between the two hospitals' neonatology departments. A young woman wanted to leave her home city, and Dalton helped make it happen.

He's been staying at an Air B&B in Denver while we looked for a rescue property. The real estate agent presented us as a couple.

And we are. I've spent as much time in LA as possible, and Dalton even made it to Boulder twice.

Maybe I should have stuck a ring on my finger and let them make an assumption.

Stan leads the other couple into the room as well. This is it. We'll find out what we're up against.

Dalton and I stand in front of the sofa but don't sit down yet. I'm ready for battle. I start mentally preparing the arguments.

Stan turns to us. "This is Lana and Jed from the Denver Post. They wanted to do a story on the history of the property before it changed hands."

Lana turns to me. "So you're going to be the new owners?"

I swivel to Dalton. It's already decided then? Our agent acted like we had to win them over. "Yes! Yes, we are!"

"Let's get a shot of the four of you," Jed says. "Maybe by the fireplace."

Stan and Maria move toward the giant stone hearth in the towering oak wood wall.

We line up beside them. Dalton puts his arm around me and squeezes.

Emotions wash over me as Jed shifts us around and takes several shots.

"Why don't we walk around while we talk?" Lana suggests.

And so we do, the six of us touring the property. We learn more about the history of the ranch, how it operated, and the challenges it faced over the decades.

Lana asks me about the plans for the rescue and promises to return when it's operational, so people will learn about it.

Eventually, Lana and Jed leave, and Stan and Maria excuse themselves. "We'll see you at closing," Stan says with a wave.

"You'll always be welcome here," I tell them. "Anytime you want to visit."

"We're going to live on cruise ships!" Maria says. "You two stay as long as you like."

The couple disappears inside the house.

Dalton and I climb the rise behind the house that

gives a view of the barns and the pastures and the mountains beyond.

"We could get married here, like Stan and Maria did," Dalton says. "Plenty of room. Get some tents."

"Oh, the Pickles always get married in one of the delis," I tell him. "I have to carry a traditional bouquet of kosher dills, and there's always a very fancy sandwich bar where you can make your own subs."

He stares at me for a minute. "Okay. When among the Pickles, be like the Pickles."

I snort-laugh and lay my head on his shoulder. "In med school, did you learn about the part of the brain that makes people gullible?"

"Oh, I'll get you for that." He tries to sweep me into his arms, but I wiggle away and take off down the other side of the hill.

He chases after me.

I shriek, running as well as I can in ballet flats. His shoes are much better for the terrain, so he easily catches me and soon I'm thrown over his shoulder. "You know what happens to cheeky women?"

I hammer his shoulder. "What happens to cheeky women?"

He slides me down his chest until I'm standing in front of him again.

"This?" He lifts my hand and slides a ring on it. The diamond sparkles in the light.

"Dalton?" I shift it around to get a better look. It's not small. "How did you manage this?"

"I don't make an intern salary anymore."

Right. The struggle will get less and less as we go.

He can help his mother. I will make real money as the head of the rescue and veterinary operation.

We made it to the other side.

I stare up at him. "Since I'm a cheeky woman, I guess I should ask if there's a question that goes with this ring?"

"There is." And he gets down on one knee, then springs back up again with a yelp. "Rock."

I laugh. "Here." We take a few steps backward to smoother ground.

"Let's try this again." He kneels carefully. "This one is good."

"You know, kneeling isn't mandatory."

"He'll think it is." Dalton aims this thumb back toward the house.

I spot Jed in the distance. I turn to see the shot he's taking. Dalton kneeling, me standing before him in a pencil skirt and flats a lot like the outfit I wore the day we met.

And spread behind us, the Colorado mountains and the flower-dotted foothills.

It will be a gorgeous photo, the two of us a small part of a very big idea, one we came up with together.

He takes my hand. "So Nadia Armstrong, lover of kittens, rescuer of all things lost and weary, beautiful and strong, love of my life, will you marry me?"

I clasp his fingers, the answer already glinting on my hand. "Yes, Dalton Murphy, doctor to the most fragile members of our human race, willing to move across three states to be with me, champion of DuckDuckJeep, giver of five-star orgasms, and love of *my* life, I will marry you."

He stands then and gathers me against him. When his face lowers to mine, our lips connecting in the kiss we both know so well, a breeze kicks up, sending flower petals scattering across the hills.

I close my eyes to the sun, the mountains, the blossoms, and think to myself, we made it. All of us. Me, Dalton, our kitties, and the animals and families who will come under our care.

We're going to do great things. I'm so blessed that we will get to do them *together*.

Love this wild Pickle family? Nadia's brother Axel is hiking naked as usual when he stumbles upon a young woman in trouble. And she also, inexplicably, *has no pants* in the hilarious Tasty Pickle.

Loved Max and Camryn and baby Esmee? (The pickle fans named her!) Read their sneaky love story, where they hide their relationship from her brother, who is Max's best friend, in the early Pickleverse with Hot Pickle.

There are over 13 books in the Pickleverse, ready whenever you need a laugh. Keep up to date with my newsletter or text list at JJKnight.com/news

CHARACTERS WITH THEIR OWN BOOKS

- **Nadia's oldest brother Rhett** gets himself in a real pickle when the assistant he fired shows up on the company cruise. They have to weather a storm in complete solitude on the deserted island in Juicy Pickle.
- **Nadia's brother Court** has a picklish situation when a woman he had a one-night stand with on New Year's Eve shows up at his office eight months pregnant. With her goat. That one's Salty Pickle.
- **Uncle Sherman** raised a whole brood of sons. Read their hilarious adventures in romance in the original Pickle trilogy: Big Pickle, Hot Pickle, and Spicy Pickle.

BOOKS BY JJ KNIGHT

Romantic Comedies

Big Pickle ~ Hot Pickle ~ Spicy Pickle

Tasty Mango ~ Tasty Pickle ~ Tasty Cherry

Royal Pickle ~ Royal Rebel ~ Royal Escape

Juicy Pickle ~ Salty Pickle ~ Hold the Pickle

Second Chance Santa

The Wedding Confession

The Wedding Shake-up

Not Exactly a Small-Town Romance

Single Dad on Top ~ The Accidental Harem

MMA Fighters

Uncaged Love ~ Fight for Her ~ Reckless Attraction

Get emails or texts from JJ about her new releases:

JJKnight.com/news

ABOUT JJ KNIGHT

 JJ Knight is one of the pen names
of six-time *USA Today* bestselling
author Deanna Roy. She lives in
Austin, Texas, with her family.

Visit her at jjknight.com.

facebook.com/jjknightauthor

instagram.com/deannaroyauthor

bookbub.com/profile/jj-knight